Improvise, Adapt, and Overcome

Zombies

Book One

A Zombie Story

By M.E. Lincoln

www.AuthorMELincoln.com

M.E. Lincoln

Part One: Improvise

Chapter One

Aurora, Colorado
Friday, May 4, 7:15pm

Victor tapped his foot in time to the music as "Free Bird" came to its crescendo in the background. What had he been talking about? Oh, yeah. America needed to see the error of its ways and he was just the patriot to show them the light.

"We need to show them all," he said, pausing to take another swig of beer. "Show America that they screwed over the wrong people. We got to make a statement. A big one."

Victor held his cards close to his chest and tapped the table with the index finger of his free hand. His gaze roamed around the room, feeling at home in his small basement bar. Here, he was king. He didn't have to worry about some uppity son-of-a-gun coming for his Confederate flag or his weapons. He could say what he wanted and not a soul would speak against him.

Not that people often spoke against Victor directly. He towered over most people, which tended to be intimidating enough. The bald head and a long salt-and-pepper goatee lent extra gravity to his scowl though, and it usually sent people in the other direction. He aimed that scowl at his only child, Chuck, who leaned forward to toss two more chips onto the pile as he grinned.

"Let's see you put your money where your mouth is, old man."

"Oh, come on, man," Chuck's friend, Bernie, groaned. "I fold."

Victor's friend, Dale, threw his cards down, too. "I'm out."

He looked down at his cards and decided to go for it. He deserved the win. He tossed his two chips in and laid down his cards with a flourish.

"Try to beat that, son."

Chuck ran a hand through his short black hair and tossed his cards down. "You've got me."

"So, how are you going to show America?" Bernie asked as he shuffled the cards.

"I don't know," Victor answered, rubbing the devil dog tattoo on his forearm. The needle had gone deep when he'd gotten the ink one drunken night back in his days as a US Marine.

It still itched sometimes. His gaze caught on the 1985 September Playboy's Playmate of the Month that had been on the wall of his basement since before his son was born. Victor had been infatuated with Venice Kong for as long as he could remember. He took another drink and let his mind wander.

Chuck slapped his hand down on the table with a loud thud. "I know what we can do!"

"Well, spit it out, kid. We ain't got all day," Dale said in annoyance when Chuck didn't elaborate.

Chuck flushed before sitting up straighter. "I work in a pharmaceutical lab. The last several batches of those drugs they've been testing killed a load of mice. Let's use them to make our statement."

"Can you really say you work in the lab if you only clean the building?" Bernie asked, smirking as he dealt another hand.

"Shut up, Bernie," Victor said.

Chuck stood up and carried his empty beer bottles across the room to join the empty pizza box and the other empties scattered across the bar. He caught sight of the muted news on the flat screen across from the leather couch and clenched his jaw.

Just like always, there was some new disaster *They* didn't want the people to know about. Not the truth, anyway. He let out a low growl of disgust when the screen switched to a commercial for one of those diet shakes.

"Seriously, how are dead mice going to make a statement?" Bernie asked, genuine confusion in his eyes.

Chuck slapped his forehead with an open palm, groaning in frustration. "We aren't going to use dead mice," he said. "We're going to use the drugs. To kill people. Like how the drugs killed the mice. Get it?"

"Ahh. Sure. What kind of drugs are they?"

"It doesn't really matter what kind of drugs they are, does it?" Chuck asked, losing his temper. "Just as long as our statement is made."

Dale sat up straighter, taking a real interest in the conversation now. "What are we going to do with the drugs? How do we use them to kill people?"

Thinking on his feet, Chuck loved how confident he sounded. "We can drop them in the water supply."

Victor raised his eyebrows in question even as he nodded in approval. "It sounds like you've already thought about this."

Chuck met his gaze. "Well, you always say we need to do something. So, let's stop talking and actually *do* it."

Chuck made and held eye contact with each of the men at the table, challenging them to speak against him.

Dale ran a hand over his smooth, bald head in a gesture they all recognized. Though Victor and Dale were in their fifties, they had a regular poker night with Chuck and Bernie. Despite being in their twenties, they usually had Friday evenings free. Dale developed a fondness for the boys and didn't want to see them do something stupid.

"Hold up there a second, son. Start with how you're going to get the drugs out of the lab. What water supply are you going to drop it in?"

Chuck shrugged. "I don't have all the answers, Dale. This is something *WE* are going to do. It always has been. We're all in this. We're going to show America the error of its ways *together*, just like we always talked about."

Dale nodded in approval. "I'm not saying it's a bad plan. I just wanted to know if you've thought that far."

Chuck smiled. "You let me worry about how to get the drugs out of the lab. I've got a plan for that. It's everything else we need to nail down."

Dale sat back and met Victor's gaze. He'd raised this boy right. Chuck had become a man of action. "I'll handle finding the best water system to release the drugs for maximum impact."

Chuck nodded. "Awesome. When I get the drugs, I'll send out a text and everyone will know to meet up here. Dad, you can drive your Equinox since it is better on gas, can fit all of us comfortably, and will handle off-road conditions if necessary."

Bernie piped up, still holding the unshuffled cards since the conversation grabbed every bit of his attention. He'd always been the chubby, uncoordinated tagalong and he wanted something real to do. "What's my part in all this?"

Chuck shrugged. "You're on chow duty, Bern. Even revolutionaries need to eat."

Bernie narrowed his eyes at Chuck. "Okay, but what do we do *after*?"

Chuck fought the urge to roll his eyes. "What do you mean after? After what?"

"Well, once you steal the drugs, the lab will call the police, and then they will go looking for you. They won't believe that you and all your known associates happened to disappear at the same time. Life here will be over for us."

"He's right," Victor said. "We'll have to pull all our cash together and find somewhere to lie low until everything blows over. Find fake identities if we have to, but I'm not sure it will come to that. We just can't use our credit cards. That's how the government will track us."

"They can use our cellphones, too," Dale added. "We'll have to ditch our phones too."

Bernie's smile faded. "Ugh. I don't want to give up my phone. Do you have any idea what level I'm on in this game I've been playing since forever?" He sighed, his shoulders slumping. "Not to mention the uber-hot girl I've been talking to on the dating app I joined a while back."

The others didn't bother to hide their contempt as they stared at Bernie. No words were needed to make him feel small. In seconds, he squirmed under their disdain.

"Fine! You can take my stupid phone!" Bernie grumped.

"Everyone turn off your cell phones when you get home tonight and *keep* them off." The others didn't even think to question the authority in Victor's voice. He'd always been the natural leader of their small group.

"Pack your go bag and be here tomorrow morning, waiting for Chuck."

Bernie's eyes widened in shock. "Hold on a minute. Just *hold on*. The way y'all are talking, it sounds like we're going to do this tomorrow."

Victor, Chuck, and Dale exchanged knowing glances.

"Well, if Chuck can get the drugs tomorrow and if Dale finds the best water source to dump them, I say we go ahead and get it done," Victor answered.

Bernie shrugged. "Well, when you put it like that," He clapped his hands together and smiled, "I guess we're really going to do this."

"You guys meet here early and get everything loaded into dad's SUV," Chuck said. "I should be able to snatch the drugs and take off before lunch, so I can be back here by eleven. We can hit the road right away and get to the water source before anyone starts looking for us."

"You two make sure you have your parts handled and everything ready before Chuck gets here. Say, by ten hundred local," Victor said.

Dale nodded. "I'll have our route marked on a map. And I have a cousin here in Aurora who will let us crash at her place until the heat dies down."

Bernie jumped to his feet, a bit unsteady after his many beers throughout the poker game. "Wait! You're talking about Wendy, aren't you? Aww, man. She's so mean. I think we need to plan this out a little better."

"Wendy aren't mean; she just doesn't like *you*," Dale said, chuckling. "If you hadn't made such a fool of yourself that summer..." Dale trailed off and took another swig of his beer, finishing the bottle and adding it to the growing pile of empties next to his chair.

Bernie sank back down into his chair, defeated. If Wendy was a secure place to stay, that's where they would go. He just didn't like the woman. She was mean as a hellcat and twice as nasty. He exasperated long and loud as he thought of being cooped up in a house with an ill-tempered woman like Wendy.

Victor ignored Bernie's antics. He didn't particularly like Wendy either, but he wouldn't turn down an isolated safehouse. "Listen up, men. We have a solid plan. Number one, get the drugs. Number two, dump the drugs into the water supply. Number three, lie low and watch the deaths on the news."

He stood up and raised his beer to the other three men. "True America, one. Unnatural America, zero!"

Their four voices cheered together, the sound filling the room for a moment.

"Well, actually," Bernie interjected. "If you want a more accurate tally, I think it's more like Unnatural Americ—"

"Shut up, Bernie!" the other three snapped in unison.

Chapter Two

Denver, Colorado
Saturday, May 5, 07:53

Chuck went to work as usual the following morning, but for him, everything had changed overnight. He walked into the pharmaceutical building the same as he did every other day, already wearing his blue coverall jumpsuit over his street clothes. He set about his normal routine cleaning each area in turn until, at last, he found himself outside the central lab.

He tried to watch a pair of scientists without being obvious. He saw one of them give a mouse a shot before placing it in a glass cage with three other mice. When he glanced back a few minutes later, the mouse was dead. The sound was muffled, but Chuck caught snippets of the scientists' conversation.

"Welp, that's definitely not the cure for Alzheimer's, the first scientist said.

"Thank you for that brilliant assessment, Liu. This batch had so much promise," the second scientist, Sauer, said as he removed his glasses and rubbed the bridge of his nose.

13

"Okay, so it's back to the drawing board. Let's go over the dosage again and see if that's where we went wrong."

Liu grimaced. "If we don't figure out something soon, the company may pull the funding for our project. Once more, into the breach," he said, glancing curiously at the custodian watching them through the lab windows.

Sauer put his glasses back on and reached for the hand sanitizer before he grabbed a fresh pair of gloves and got back to work. In the hall, Chuck's gaze darted around, looking for a way to clear the lab. Everything he needed was *right there,* and only those two fragile-looking scientists stood in his way.

He spotted the fire alarm next to the double doors to the lab and a plan started to form in his mind. Improvise. Adapt. Overcome. Those were the words drilled into him from childhood. The way to survive any situation. Chuck was very much his father's son, and he'd taken the Marine's message to heart.

Chuck pushed his janitorial cart nonchalantly across the room, acting as casual as possible so he didn't draw any unwanted attention. Once he'd parked the cart next to the fire alarm, he picked up a long-handled push broom and a pair of silver coffee thermoses he'd bought specially for this.

He looked around to make sure no one could see him and pulled the fire alarm before dashing behind a pillar where he'd be hidden from sight. The blaring alarm echoed off sterile lab walls and sent stabbing pains into Chuck's ears, but seeing the scientists set down their equipment and dash out of the building made it all worthwhile.

As the door was closing, Chuck stepped forward to wedge his broom through the ever-shrinking gap. It was solid enough to buy him a minute or two, at least. With the confusion from the alarm, he hoped it was all he'd need. He turned and rushed into the lab. Chuck didn't exactly know what he was looking for, but he only had a few minutes until they knew there was no fire and came back to the lab. He had to hurry.

Chuck opened the first thermos and started pouring in every liquid he could find on the lab tables. His eyes watered from the noxious smell coming from the thermos, but he didn't have time to worry about it. He just had to get the stuff and get out. Then it would be someone else's job to worry about what it was. He glanced behind him after emptying each vial, expecting to see someone staring with accusation in their eyes each time, but he was alone.

When the first thermos was nearly filled, Chuck carefully tightened the lid and opened the second. This one had a tiny bit of coffee in it, but Chuck ignored that. Surely a little coffee wouldn't hurt the cocktail of deadly chemicals. He made his way across the lab to a cabinet holding vials of liquid in a variety of colors. Chuck started grabbing them and popping the tops to pour them into the thermos. He dropped the empty tubes on the floor, where the glass shattered into a large pile by the time he'd filled the second vessel.

Smooth as butter, he removed the broom, set it next to the cart, and hurried to join the others outside. He found all the other employees gathered at the staging area in front of the building. Chuck nodded to a few people he knew, fading into the crowd before slipping away to the parking lot. He trotted over to his car, getting in as if nothing was amiss and he was just leaving for lunch. He didn't see anyone glancing his way and figured he was in the clear.

Both thermoses were secured safely in the cup holders before he reversed and took the lesser-used back entrance out of the parking lot, humming the jingle from the nutritional meal replacement commercial on the radio.

Less than five minutes later, the firefighters who'd responded to the alarm declared there was no danger and let the employees back inside the building. While the fire chief spoke with the building manager, Liu and Sauer made their way back to the Alzheimer's research lab.

Sauer went through the door first and stopped short, leaving Liu to run into his back.

"Ow! What is your problem, Sauer?"

The other scientist gestured around the lab. "What the hell happened in here, Liu? Where is everything? The firefighters wouldn't come in here if there was no fire and they certainly wouldn't trash our lab," he said, pointing to the pile of shattered test tubes and specimen vials near the storage cabinet.

"They wouldn't even be able to get in. The doors closed behind us and there's fire suppression protections built-in to each lab," Liu replied, his uneasiness growing.

17

"Something is wrong. Even if the firefighters could and did come in here, they would have no reason to touch or take our compounds."

The pair agreed and decided to take the issue to their boss, Dr. Ray. As expected, he wasn't thrilled to hear that several drug compounds were missing from the Alzheimer's lab after the unplanned fire alarm.

"Make a list of everything that's missing and report back to me. I'll get security involved in the meantime," Dr. Ray ordered, dismissing them with a wave of his hand as he turned back to the paperwork littering his desk.

About thirty minutes later, Chuck pulled up to his father's house in Aurora. Victor waited on the porch, chatting with Bernie. Chuck climbed out of the car, hoisting the twin thermoses over his head in triumph. He kicked the car door closed and strode toward the porch with a grin on his face. As he reached the top step, Dale stepped out the front door and lifted his thermos of coffee in a salute. Then he set it down on a side table.

"Maybe I'll just leave this here. We don't want any unfortunate mistakes thinking that junk is coffee," Dale said.

Victor laughed. "Probably not the worst idea you've ever had."

"No, that would have been skinny dipping with the Sanderson twins the summer of '82. I thought I'd never get rid of that poison ivy," Dale answered, laughing along with his friend.

Chuck grinned at his father as he reached the top of the porch steps. "How are we doing this fine afternoon, gentlemen?"

Dale looked at his watch. "Right on time. I thought for sure you'd be late. You run into any trouble getting those, boy?"

"Nope," he said, holding the thermoses up for everyone to see. "Not a single problem. In and out on stealth mode. Do you have the destination?"

Dale nodded. "It's a little bit of a ways away, but you're going to love it."

Chuck turned to Bernie. "Did you get enough rations to last a while?"

"Yep. I got a whole bunch of MREs for the long term and a cooler with all the best eats for the next few days. It's already stashed in the back of your dad's vehicle," Bernie said.

"Nice. Good work, man," Chuck said. He passed the thermoses to Bernie. "Go put these in there, too. Make sure they are safe."

Bernie gave Chuck a severe look, letting him know he understand the importance of the task.

He nodded and jogged off to the SUV, securing the thermoses in the back seat.

Chuck slipped off his coveralls and tossed them into his car before grabbing his go bag and adding it to the gear in Victor's vehicle. Within a few minutes of Chuck's arrival, the group was loaded into the vehicle and ready to go do their part to guide America back to where it should be.

Victor hesitated with his hand on the ignition. He turned to look at each of the men with him. Each smiled or nodded to show they were still with him, still dedicated to this course of action. Victor grinned and fired up the engine. He reversed out of his driveway and shot off down the road toward their life-changing destination.

Back at Chuck's former place of employment, Dr. Ray called the research scientists into his office. He sat ramrod straight in his chair when Liu and Sauer approached and hung up the phone as they entered. He held out his hand for the list he'd requested.

"Is this everything missing or destroyed in the lab during today's false alarm?" Dr. Ray demanded, flipping through the pages of the report Sauer had given him.

"Does this include any kind of information on what those drugs and drug combinations could do?"

Liu cleared his throat uncomfortably. "All of these drugs had an...adverse reaction."

Dr. Ray raised his eyebrows in question. "Oh? How so?"

"Each of these has resulted in death in each subject we tested," Sauer replied, glancing from Dr. Ray to Liu, who looked crushed. "We haven't been able to get any further than that, so far."

Dr. Ray continued to look unimpressed, so Sauer continued. "Which isn't at all unusual in research pharmaceuticals. This is Alzheimer's we're trying to cure. It doesn't happen overnight."

Running a hand through his dark, curly hair, Dr. Ray stood up and glared at the pair of nervous scientists. "Except it wasn't the lab developing erectile dysfunction pills that was robbed, was it?" His tone was curt and brooked no argument. "It was *your* lab. Full of failed Alzheimer's drugs. Maybe they failed *separately* but have a different effect when combined. I doubt you two were close enough to any breakthroughs to warrant intellectual espionage for any single compound.

If this is the precursor to some kind of terrorist attack, we need to know yesterday. I need to know what someone could do with those compounds."

"I don't know why someone would want to steal failed drugs," Liu admitted. "And most of the containers were left behind. If all of it were mixed together, it could be anything from the next super-virus to inert sludge, sir. And without knowing how it was mixed, we really have no way to know what the original compounds have become."

Dr. Ray pressed his fingertips together. "Whatever the reason for the theft, I have the head of security reviewing the tapes to see if we caught evidence of who was in the lab. I don't want to call in the FBI if your stuff was borrowed by another scientist or something. We deal with this in-house if possible. I'd rather the police didn't poke their noses around our business."

He ushered the two scientists out of his office and down the hall before taking the stairs down to the security office on the main floor.

"O'Connell," Dr. Ray called as he opened the door.

Two of the younger guards jumped up from the table and stood at attention as Dr. Ray crossed to rap quickly on the Head of Security's office door.

Dr. Ray didn't wait for an invitation and strode in to find a harried O'Connell watching CCTV video clips on his computer.

"I need to know who was in the central research lab. Some of our more… experimental compounds have been stolen. I don't know who. I don't know why. But I do need answers," Dr. Ray said, dropping the report of the chemicals on the Security Chief's desk.

He picked up the papers and flipped through the report, refusing to admit he didn't know what any of it meant in front of the pompous research director. He dropped it back onto the desk and turned to his computer.

"Obviously, the theft occurred during the fire alarm earlier today." O'Connell said. "You don't run cameras inside any of the labs, but I was able to get confirmation of the person who entered while the building was empty."

His fingers danced across the keyboard, and he brought up a view outside the Alzheimer's lab. With a few clicks, he'd isolated an image of Chuck's face as he stood outside, staring at Liu while he worked. O'Connell turned the monitor to share the view with Dr. Ray.

"Well, that's suspicious," Dr. Ray said of the first video clip.

"That's not all this creep did," he muttered. O'Connell hit play and they both watched Chuck pull the fire alarm, wedge the door open with a broom, and disappear into the lab with two thermoses. The security chief managed to trace Chuck on camera all the way to the parking lot. "It was the custodian. What do those drugs do, anyway?"

"They're meant to cure Alzheimer's, but some of the compounds had unexpected results and the test subjects died. According to my researchers, all of them were failures." Dr. Ray paced the small office in frustration. "I just don't see why anyone would want to steal them at this stage of development. It doesn't make any sense. Where is the value?"

"Whatever he's up to, it's no good," O'Connell said. He opened a large gray metal filing cabinet in the corner and searched employee files until he found Chuck's. "Ah, here you are, dirtbag."

Dr. Ray snatched the file from O'Connell's hands. "I'll call the police from my office.

Chapter Three

Bellvue, Colorado
Saturday, May 5, 12:40

Victor's super-duty SUV ate up the miles as they followed Dale's directions away from Aurora and up into the mountains.

"This is some nice scenery up here," Bernie said, watching the landscape through the window.

Chuck leaned his head back against the headrest and fought his boredom. "This is such a long car ride. Three and a half hours shouldn't be that long, but it feels like we have been in here for about a week. How much further, Dale?"

"An hour and fifty minutes," Dale replied, trying not to lose patience with the kid's constant complaining about the drive. Everyone just wanted instant gratification nowadays.

Victor smiled, just happy to be taking action with the only men in the world he felt he could truly trust. "On the bright side, at least there aren't too many cars out. You know the highways can turn into a parking lot if you hit them at the wrong time of day."

"Where did you say we were going, Dale?" Chuck asked.

Dale turned to look at Chuck. "I didn't and not one of you bothered to ask. We jumped in and I just started giving directions." He let out a laugh. "The name of the place is La Poudre Pass."

Chuck groaned theatrically. "I know the place. Wasn't there anywhere closer?" He tried and failed to hold back the whine in his voice.

"Quiet, boy. I picked La Poudre Pass as the best place to dump the drugs because that's where the Colorado River begins. Other than Colorado, the river supplies water to upper Wyoming, Utah, New Mexico, lower Nevada, California, and Arizona."

"Whew. That'll get the drugs far," Chuck conceded.

Victor growled in frustration as the car in front of him slowed down below the speed limit but refused to move to the slow lane.

"That's not all," Dale continued, pride clear in his voice. "It flows down to Mexico, hitting two states in the north. We wanted to make a statement and dumping the drugs at La Poudre Pass is the way to do it. Whatever's gonna happen, it's best to start at the top."

Victor's brows furrowed as he threw up a hand to gesture at the vehicle ahead of him. "The twists and turns aren't so bad. But having to drive thirty-five on the highway is making me crazy. Why won't this car in front of me just move over and let me by?"

They passed a sign ordering slow vehicles to move over for faster traffic and Victor pointed at it. "See! This car needs to pull over. I'm going to have to go around."

"It seems like there's closed gates preventing vehicles from crossing a few bridges and some of the side roads." Bernie said, though no one paid attention to him as they all voiced their opinions on slow drivers.

Chuck checked the map against the sign they just passed and saw there were roughly forty miles left. More time passed, but he kept his mouth shut. Maybe something like this was supposed to be uncomfortable.

"If we weren't on our way to commit mass murder, I'd suggest we stop and grab a beer at that bar we just passed up," Victor said. He shrugged. "Maybe on the way back."

"How many people do you think these drugs will kill?" Dale asked.

"I don't really know," Chuck said.

"Just a tiny dose was enough to kill the mice in minutes. We'll just have to sit back and wait for the results."

"Hey, check it out," Bernie said excitedly, pointing out the window. "There's a garage built into that hill.

The others glanced, but since they saw no relevance to their current mission, they ignored Bernie's sightseeing. Chuck sighed and reached behind him for the cooler full of snacks. He pulled out food and drinks for everyone and passed them out. They might as well be comfortable. They still had a while to drive.

About an hour later, Chuck grinned and pointed to the sign for Long Draw Road. Victor slowed down to make a left turn onto the road while Dale checked the map again.

"There's just twelve miles left," Dale announced.

The young guys in the SUV looked towards the road and smiled, but those smiles faded as Victor pulled to a stop in front of a closed iron gate barring the road, a thick forest on either side of the road.

"What the hell?" Chuck asked. "This is supposed to be a public road."

Victor narrowed his eyes and glared at Dale, who threw up his hands and banged his fist against the door.

"How was I supposed to know there would be a gate here? For crying out loud! As Chuck said, this is a public road."

Victor put the SUV in park and got out to examine the gate. The others jumped out and they gathered around a sign declaring the road closed. Chuck kicked a piece of litter on the side of the road and cursed.

"It must have something to do with the time of year," Bernie said.

"Well, what are we gonna do now?" Chuck demanded; his face turned flushed as he shook his fists.

"Everyone just calm down," said Victor. "The road is closed, and we have twelve miles left to go. Focusing on the problem won't get us any closer to a solution. Good enthusiasm, poor judgment, son. What do I always say?"

Chuck nodded his acknowledgment of his father's words. "Improvise. Adapt. Overcome."

"We could walk the twelve miles," Dale suggested.

Bernie groaned. "I'd really rather not walk it. That's twenty-four miles round trip."

"We can't leave my SUV out here in the open that long anyway," Victor said. "Someone would call it in, and the police would show up. We can't have that."

Dale walked back to the vehicle, grabbing the map to spread across the hood. "Let me check the map and see what our options are. I'll find a backup site in the area."

Chuck sighed, suddenly feeling exhausted with all of it. His adrenaline had been running high since early that morning and he felt like crashing hard. "Let's just dump the drugs into the river we saw driving up here and stop by that bar for a beer."

Dale held up his hand to stop Chuck. "Now just hang on a dang minute. Let me look over the map. We aren't taking the easy way out now, boy."

The others gave him a few minutes of silence to examine the map for an alternate route.

He finally looked up with a smile. "It looks like the next closest site with maximum impact is Lake Granby," Dale said. "The smaller waterway back along the route we took is Joe Wright Creek. It looks like it might eventually dump into La Poudre Pass Lake, but I think we should go to Lake Granby just to be sure."

"What makes Granby the better choice?" Victor asked.

Dale folded the map.

"The Colorado River feeds into it and picks back up going south. The water system supplies nine states, including the two in Mexico."

"We don't even know how many people are gonna die from these drugs," Bernie said. "Hell, they might not even die. They could just get sick. If the drugs get too diluted, they might not affect anyone."

Chuck shook his head. "I don't believe that. I'm positive we can get at least a couple dozen with them. How many people live up here? Let's just dump them in the creek."

"No," Victor said as he shook his head. "That implies a target on this area. It's America we want to get the message. Not some piddly little community in rural Colorado. We go to Lake Granby. It will take longer, but the strength of our statement will be worth it. If anything, we'll make the people of Granby really sick and then people will realize how easy it is to target the nation's water supply. They'll see how vulnerable they are. Improvise. Adapt. Overcome, gentlemen. Back in the SUV."

Chuck looked at his shoes to avoid meeting his father's gaze and the disappointment he was certain he'd see. "Yeah, you're right, dad."

"You're darn right, I'm right," Victor said, climbing into the driver's seat once more.

Part Two: Adapt

Chapter Four

Lake Granby, Colorado

Saturday, May 5, 17:37

The men stayed silent for most of the remaining drive to Lake Granby. They all let their minds wander to the effects their actions would bring. Half-formed plans of how they would take control during the ensuing chaos filled their thoughts as they moved closer to the point of no return. Everything would change forever after they did this. Everything, one way or another.

"Okay, we're here, but I think we should dump them where Lake Granby ends and the Colorado River picks up," Dale said. "Drive a little further, Victor. There will be a bridge as the divider."

Victor nodded.

"There haven't been many other cars out for this time of year. I think we can get in and out unseen."

Chuck's body buzzed with excitement, and he held one of the thermoses tightly as the bridge came into view. Finally, they were going to *do something.* All his life, his father had talked about how it was their duty as good, strong American men to step up and do something to guide the country back to where it belonged.

Victor saw an excellent parking spot along the tree line just before the bridge. He checked his mirrors to make sure the roads were still empty and pulled a U-turn. He parked and shut off the SUV, then turned to face his companions.

"This is it, men. Today, we take the first step toward a new America. A better America," Victor said. He took a deep breath and let it out slowly. "Let's go."

They got out of the SUV, with Chuck and Bernie each carrying one of the thermoses full of stolen drugs.

They walked down the sloped bank beside the bridge to the water's edge. A gentle breeze blew the dark hair from Chuck's forehead and the sun shone on the bald heads of the older men. Bernie stood clutching his thermos close to his chest.

"Should we say a speech or something before we dump them in?" Bernie asked.

"Why?" Chuck asked.

"Well... We are about to kill maybe a few dozen people, a whole town if we're lucky," Bernie said with a shrug. "And possibly make a lot of people in nine states very sick if we're fortunate. It just kind of feels like we should say *something*."

"You know what, you're right," Victor said. "I've got this. Here's to all the bastards that are about to finally get what's coming to them. Here's to our statement. Here's to what happens when you screw over people like us, America!"

"Amen, brother," Dale said, patting Victor on the shoulder.

Victor turned to Chuck and Bernie, then pointed to the lake. "It's time, boys."

They walked as close to under the bridge as possible. Chuck and Bernie opened the thermoses and dumped the contents into the water while Victor and Dale kept watch for any possible observers.

"The thermoses will float, so we can drop them in some bushes on our way back to the SUV. Wipe them down with your shirts so there's no fingerprints, boys," Victor said when the younger men had delivered their payload.

"Well, that's that," Dale said as Chuck and Bernie carried out their instructions. "All that's left is to head over to Wendy's place in Aurora and lay low there until the heat dies down."

The men started to walk back to the Equinox, but Bernie lagged behind, taking a few minutes to stretch his legs and take in the scenery. He took a deep breath and made his way back to the SUV as well.

The group stopped for gas and then continued on their way. Chuck watched the people on the street through the window as they drove. He felt anger rise in his chest.

"Look at these pretentious a-holes," Chuck said, his voice practically dripping the venom he felt. "I hope they're the first to die."

"Well, if they live around here, there's a good chance they just might be," Dale said, grinning. "Hopefully along with every idiot who drives slow in the fast lane."

"I can't wait to get to your cousin's and have a nice, cold beer, Dale," Victor said. "What do you think she's making for dinner?"

"Probably something easy, like tacos," Dale answered.

"Beer and tacos?" Bernie said with delight. "That sounds delicious."

Aurora, Colorado

Saturday, May 5, 19:49

Wendy lived near the mall and had all the lights on to welcome them when they arrived at her house. A few seconds after Victor turned into the driveway, the garage door started opening. He pulled the SUV into the garage, and they all saw Wendy standing at the door into the house. Victor shut off the vehicle and they all climbed out to greet their host.

They grabbed their bug out bags and followed Wendy into the house, where the air did indeed smell of tacos. She showed them where to put their things in the two spare bedrooms she had to offer and left them to wash up while she served dinner. By the time they emerged into the sparsely furnished but meticulously clean dining room to eat, Wendy had the table loaded with taco fixings and chilled beer. The men dove into the food, practically inhaling it. The excitement of the day had built a fierce appetite in all of them.

While they ate and drank their beer, the men took turns giving Wendy an account of their day. The usual animosity between Wendy and Bernie was gone. It seemed she finally saw him as someone who could be useful.

"There's extra water in the pantry," Wendy said. "And there's more in the basement."

"Good. I don't think we should bathe in the water," Bernie said.

Wendy's jaw dropped. "Not bathe! How do you expect us to manage that?" Her tone had her usual disdain for Bernie.

"Well, the drugs we dumped in the water can kill you, Wendy, so it's probably best *not* to get it on your skin," Bernie said, not bothering to hide his sarcasm. "You remember Flint, Michigan, right?" He leaned forward in his chair, seeing he'd captured their full attention. "The news said they shouldn't drink or even bathe in the water. And that was just bad lead pipes or something."

Wendy reached out a hand to Dale's shoulder, her face a mask of concern. "Does Aurora even get its water from the Colorado River? There's a lot of good people here I need to warn if it does."

Dale patted her hand. "Don't worry, Wendy. Aurora should be safe. I checked. All the same, I'd rather we not take the chance. If for some reason the drugs spread further than we think and you were to get sick or God forbid, die... Well, that would be on us, wouldn't it? You aren't like the others, the ones we're using as pons to make our statement." Dale held her gaze, his expression serious. "Let's just use the bottled water to wash up for a while, alright?"

Wendy sighed but knew better than to question Dale more than once. "Well, alright. I suppose, if need be, I can go out and get more bottled water. It's not like any of you will be able to leave for a while."

When they'd finished eating, the guys got up from the table and turned toward the television, leaving their mess behind.

40

"Hey!" Wendy yelled. "I don't know where y'all think you are, but you better get back here and clean up after yourselves. There's dish soap and a sponge by the sink. I agreed to let you stay in my home. I did not agree to wait on you hand and foot. I cooked. You clean."

Chuck looked over at Bernie and rolled his eyes. Wendy saw it and glared at him. "Do you have something you'd like to say, *Chuck?*"

Something about the way she emphasized his name made Chuck's eyes go wide with panic when she stood up to follow them if they didn't stop. He shook his head.

Bernie met Chuck's gaze and shook his head. "Let's just do the dishes, man. She's not asking for much."

Chuck groaned but turned away to help his friend clear the table. Wendy joined the older men in the living room, where they were flipping through the news channels.

"Authorities in Denver, Colorado are searching for this man, Charles "Chuck" Kane. He is wanted for questioning concerning a robbery at a pharmaceutical research facility that took place on Saturday at his place of employment in Denver."

"Turn it up, that's me!" Chuck cried from the kitchen as he washed the dishes. His employee ID photo appeared on the screen.

"Police say they have video evidence that proves Kane stole an unspecified amount of unregulated drug compounds from the facility after pulling a fire alarm to empty the building. Authorities have been unable to locate Kane to determine his intentions or the whereabouts of the stolen drugs."

"Well, they didn't mention any of us yet," Dale said. "I say we keep monitoring for the time being, but it seems like all the heat is on Chuckie boy here. If need be, the rest of us should be able to leave the house for supplies."

"Chuck is on house arrest until things calm down for sure," Victor said.

"The news will move on to the illnesses soon, and people will be so occupied that they will forget about Chuck. And they may not have mentioned it, but I'm sure the cops are looking for me, too. If they're advertising for help from the public, they have already looked for information from his known associates."

Wendy scoffed. "You all didn't rob a bank. I promise you're not a high priority for the Aurora police department. They got better things to do, and no one knows you're here. Relax."

"Still, we stay put. We brought enough supplies that we shouldn't have to leave for a while anyway," Victor said.

"It's late," Wendy said, her tone soothing. "Let's all turn in for the night and come at this again after a good night's rest. We'll see what the news says tomorrow."

Chapter Five

Aurora, Colorado

Tuesday, May 8, 17:30

As the days passed, hundreds of people from all over the world visited Colorado to take part in countless tourist activities. Alongside the tourists, hundreds of thousands used and consumed water from the Colorado River. Those people continued to live and work, as usual, many of them flying home to continue their lives back in their home states or countries. Businesses opened. Goods were shipped. Four full days after the drugs were dumped in the water, and no one seemed to know anything.

Things inside Wendy's house were as normal as they could be. The men were slightly dejected that nothing seemed to be happening yet, but they held onto their faith that America would get their message.

After a long day at work, Wendy arrived home tired and opened the door to find the guys had cleaned the house while she was gone.

"Thanks for picking up the house, guys," she said as she dropped her purse and keys on the table by the front door.

"It's not a problem at all, Wendy," Bernie said, hoping to earn some extra points with her. "Thanks for letting us stay with you. How about we order pizza tonight?"

Wendy sighed in agreement. Dinner she didn't have to cook or clean up after sounded perfect. "Yes. Please. You order. I need a shower." She dug out her credit card and passed it over to Bernie before retreating toward her room.

Bernie's voice stopped her. "Wait! You can't take a shower, Wendy. We poisoned the water, remember?"

She whirled around, losing what little patience she had left. "Look. I've had a long, hard day. We were short-handed and I worked my butt off today.

I can't just wash up. I need a dang shower and I'm going to take one. Nothing has happened here, and Dale said Aurora isn't even on the same water system as the Colorado River!"

Her voice rose with each word and soon Bernie was shrinking back from her unleashed anger and frustration. "I-I'm sure it will be okay. I just wanted to be on the safe side."

Wendy rolled her eyes. "Thank you for your concern, Bernie. I'll be fine." She made her way to the master suite without another word, slamming the door behind her before starting the water for a long, luxurious hot shower.

Victor shrugged and turned his attention back to the news, where the others soon joined him.

Granby, Colorado

Friday, May 11, 18:15

A middle-aged man sat at the dining table with his wife after finishing dinner, one hand supporting his head while the other rubbed his sore throat.

"Carl, maybe we should take you to see Dr. Hutchins?" his wife, Tonya said as she put a loving hand on his shoulder.

He waved the idea away. "No. That's not necessary. This new diet just doesn't agree with me. I just need some rest. If it's this bad in the morning, I promise I'll call in sick."

Tonya sighed. "I'll give you tonight, but that's it. I know you don't like going to the doctor, honey. But if TheraFlu and a hot toddy don't kick it, you're going."

"Okay. How about I just sit and relax in front of the TV for a bit?" Carl suggested, his voice softer and rougher than usual.

"You do that. I'll clean up dinner and make you that hot toddy," Tonya answered.

Carl moved slowly to the living room and collapsed into his favorite recliner. He felt terrible. Any minute, his guts were going to erupt from his body all over their living room.

He flipped the TV to a random channel and relaxed into the chair. He drifted into an uneasy sleep within minutes.

Tonya put on the kettle, humming a song she'd had stuck in her head as she cleared the dinner dishes away and loaded the dishwasher. When the kettle whistled, she made the drink for Carl and added a few saltine crackers to the plate before taking it to him.

She set the cup and saucer on the side table and reached out to shake Carl's shoulder. He flopped back into the chair at her touch, slumping over lifelessly. His pale skin had a deathly pallor, and his lips were tinted blue. The irises of his still open eyes had gone white.

"Carl! Oh my God, no!" Tonya cried, pulling her hand back from the coolness of his skin.

His white irises focused on her, and Carl leaped from the recliner. He grasped wildly and grabbed Tonya around the shoulders. She gasped in shock; certain he'd been dead only moments ago.

"Carl, what are you doing?" she screamed when he tried to bite her neck.

Tonya put an arm against his chest and tried to push him away. He lunged forward again, and his teeth connected with her shoulder, ripping out a chunk of flesh. She shrieked in pain as he chewed the bite, her fresh blood rolling down his chin. Horror filled her as she saw none of the man she'd shared her life with inside the monster who attacked her.

She struggled to get free of him while he was distracted. Tears streamed down her cheeks as she struggled to make sense of everything. How had her husband's loving hands changed into grasping claws? When did the mouth that had given her so many sweet kisses transform into that ravening maw?

Tonya ran into the kitchen and grabbed the first weapon she could find, a long, sturdy kitchen knife. She spun around to find Carl right behind her. She panicked and stabbed him in the heart—but he *didn't react.*

He reached for her, grabbing her injured shoulder with one hand and a fistful of her hair with the other. She pushed against his chest again, but he turned his attention to snapping at anything he could reach with his teeth.

She kicked him in his bad knee and Carl collapsed, losing his grip on her. She darted forward while he was off balance and brought her knife down on the top of his head. The knife sunk into his flesh far easier than she'd thought it would and the blade sank to the hilt. Carl fell to the kitchen floor with a hard thud and didn't move. Tonya stood over his body in utter shock.

She bit back a scream, knowing she wouldn't stop if she started. She grabbed a dishtowel from the counter and ran down the hall, snatching her keys from the table by the front door. With a last horrified look down the hall to the kitchen, Tonya ran out of the house.

Outside, she saw pure chaos everywhere she looked. Across the street, the neighbor's eight-year-old twin boys were eating their father. Just an hour ago, she'd seen them playing catch on that same front lawn.

One tore greedily at his throat while the other gnawed on his legs. Their mother ran outside screaming as she tried to pull her children off her bleeding husband.

"What have you done? Marcus, Elliott, stop this!" she screamed.

One of them, Tonya could never tell them apart, let go of their father and dove for their mother's legs. The child bit a chunk from her ankle, and she fell to the ground screaming. She tried to fight the boys off, but she couldn't run and didn't want to hurt them. She screamed for help when she saw her husband getting to his feet. The other boy lunged for her neck and her screams were soon cut off as gurgles of blood filled her throat and the boys' father joined them in the feasting.

Screams of horror and pain rang out from almost every house and the bloody scenes had spilled out onto the street in many places. Tim, her neighbor to her left, ran out of his house, holding his bleeding arm. He looked around, confused, and saw Tonya standing in her yard in shock. Tim darted over to her.

"We need to go!" Tim yelled. When she didn't respond, he grabbed her shoulders and shook her. "Tonya, we need to go now! We can't stay here.

She shrieked when he grabbed her shoulder and snapped back to her surroundings. Tonya didn't resist when he took her keys and pushed her toward her car.

"Get in, I'll drive." Tim yelled. "We need to go now!"

"What is happening?" Tonya said, her voice quivered with fear and confusion, her eyes glazed with pain yet still moved on auto pilot towards the passenger seat of her car.

Tim's wife, Barbara, appeared at their house. She looked over and saw Tim and Tonya heading for the car, then she started sprinting towards them. Tim hopped in the driver's seat and struggled to get the key into the ignition. Tonya's eyes widened as she noticed the distance between her and Barbara diminishing.

Barbara had the same pale skin, blue lips, and white irises her Carl had. Tonya hastily got into the car but didn't pull her leg in fast enough before Barbara slammed into the door.

Tonya shrieked. Tim finally got the key into the ignition and the engine roared to life. He popped the gearshift into reverse and stomped on the gas pedal, hastily reversing towards the road, but Barbara gripped the car door before it was out of her grasp and held on while getting dragged.

Tonya watched in horror and amazement as Barbara gnawed at the other side of the window, unable to get to her. Tim then jerked the wheel to the left which caused Barbara to lose her grip while Tonya grabbed for the center console. Pain radiated throughout her whole body. Once in the road, Tim slammed on the brakes. Barbara lost her grip on the car door and ended up landing in the street in front of the passenger side tire.

Tonya frantically pulled her leg inside the car, closed the car door, and put on her seatbelt. She panted from pain and exertion as Tim cried silently when he heard the telltale crunch of his wife's skull when the car drove over her. Tim wiped his eyes with his still bleeding arm and kept driving with a white-knuckle grip on the steering wheel.

Tonya stared in horrified fascination at the scenes of carnage they passed as they fled the neighborhood. She watched a couple frantically trying to get into their car. The husband was fighting off their teenage son while trying to get into the driver side seat. The wife slammed the passenger door behind her when she saw two more crazed people run toward her side of the car. The crazed people ran up and started beating on the window. The woman screamed. She then climbed over to the driver side seat and took the keys out of her husband's hand. The husband looked at her, wide eyed and franticly shook his head. The woman started the car and threw the car into drive, leaving her husband standing in shock. Tonya winced when the teenager pounced and bit into his back. Before he even had a chance to react, the other two had tackled him to the ground and feasted on his flesh.

"My God, Tim. They are *eating* each other!" Tonya said.

Tim swerved to avoid a collision with another car fleeing in the opposite direction. On each street, the muffled screams from the houses around them pulled their nerves ever tighter.

They rounded another corner and Tonya fought the urge to vomit as they saw two children eating another child on the playground. Everywhere she looked, people ran from their homes screaming as they tried to get away from the loved ones who now wanted to eat them. Time and again, she saw them get caught by someone else.

Tim tried valiantly to avoid the other vehicles on the road as he crossed over East Grant Ave. He passed a car going the opposite direction, the driver fighting off a ravenous passenger. Blood splattered the car's windshield as it swerved wildly, before jumping the curb and hitting a light pole. Tim jerked the wheel the other direction to avoid a wreck and smashed into a white-eyed crazy as he crossed over East Grant Ave. He kept driving.

He narrowly avoided a runaway truck as he worked his way closer to Hwy 40. He tried to numb himself to the horror all around him. "It's like… It's like they've turned into zombies," Tim whispered, unable to make himself believe this was reality.

Tonya moaned in pain as he swerved to avoid more people on the road.

People with white eyes and blood dripping from their mouths. But zombies weren't real. "This isn't a video game, Tim."

He drove around a pack of people and another car accident to finally pull into the parking lot of Middle Park Health. The drive had only been a few minutes, but it had felt like hours to the traumatized occupants of the car. He looked over at Tonya and saw how pale she was from the blood loss. He drove right up to the emergency room entrance and parked.

"We need help!" he screamed as he ran around the car to help Tonya.

Tonya unbuckled her seatbelt. Tim pulled one of her arms around his shoulder and helped her out of the car. Tonya moved sluggishly as if she struggled for even the smallest bit of energy. She'd lost so much blood. He half dragged her toward the hospital.

Everything at the hospital seemed calm to Tim, and he found a huge disconnect to the chaos just one street away. Any minute they would be swarmed.

Inside the hospital, Dr. Brian Jacobs sat in his office, catching up on his charting. Two nurses sat at the nurse's station. He'd requested Nurse Dee be the charge nurse years ago due to her compassion and years of experience, although, those two acted more like brother and sister than colleagues. Dee spent her time catching up on company mandatory quarterly learning modules while Nurse Ana caught up on company emails. Through the open door, Dr. Jacobs could hear them chatting.

"My goodness, it's slow tonight," said Ana.

Dee shushed. "Never say the 'S' or the 'Q' word here. Now we're going to get slammed."

Ana laughed. "You're just being superstitious."

Dee shook a finger at her. "You'll see. It's not superstition if it's true. Just you wait." She raised her eyebrows and tilted her head toward the door.

Just then, Tim burst into the ER with Tonya sagging by his side.

"We need help! Please!" Tim screamed as Tonya collapsed in his arms.

Dee crossed her arms and breathed an exaggerated sigh. Ana grimaced.

"Yeah, yeah. I know. You told me."

Dr. Jacobs ran out to help the two nurses. They grabbed a clean gurney and raced toward the patients. Tonya mumbled constantly, but her words were so slurred no one could understand her. Tim rambled about people losing their minds and turning into zombies all over the city. He grew agitated when it was clear they didn't believe him.

"This is real, and they're coming. We'll be swarmed any minute now. You must prepare. You don't understand. These things are *eating people!*" Tim shouted. "You gotta listen to me!"

Dr. Jacobs ordered a sedative for their obviously distraught patient. The drugs sent him to sleep in seconds and left the medical staff free to treat the bleeding wound on his arm. Tonya had fallen into unconsciousness and didn't fight them as they stopped her bleeding.

With the emergency over, the patients were tucked into separate rooms to be monitored until they woke up and could explain what happened to them.

"Dr. Jacobs, I'm not getting any answer from the police station. I tried to report whatever crime these two suffered, but the line is busy. I called five times," Ana said from the nurse's station.

Dee heard the alarms from the monitors in Tim's room go off. She ran in and found he was not breathing, his skin pale and his lips blue. She checked for a pulse. There was none. "Brian! The patient's coding! We need a crash cart in here!" she yelled, hitting the button for a code and started chest compressions.

The doctor ran in with the crash cart and turned on the defibrillator. Tim sat up. Dee smiled, but only for a moment. Tim thrusted himself toward the unsuspecting woman, biting and snapping at the air as she fought him off. Dr. Jacobs grabbed Tim and pulled him away from the nurse, knocking the man back.

Ana called hospital security and watched with wide eyes from the nurse's station, knowing she would only be in the way in the small room. Out in the lobby, Officer Dale Patterson arrived at the ER and crossed over to speak with Ana.

"The chief sent me over, there's some kind of plague in town."

Ana pointed into the patient room, where Tim rose to his feet. "Forget that. You gotta help them! Now!"

Officer Patterson hurried to the room and saw Tim fighting to take a chunk out of anyone he could reach. Officer Patterson drew his gun. "Stop where you are," he ordered.

Tim didn't stop, but he did turn toward Officer Patterson instead. "I said freeze."

While he was distracted, Dr. Jacobs and Dee tried to slip out of the room, leaving the officer to handle the situation without them in the way. Tim sprang forward for the officer, no humanity in his eyes. The cop rolled the crash cart into Tim's path, and it ended up hitting Tim in the chest. The momentum of the crash cart knocked Tim off balance, and he fell.

They all heard the sickening crunch of bone as his wrist snapped, but Tim didn't appear to notice. He rose again and lunged toward the door where Officer Patterson stood along with the hospital staff behind him, watching in terror.

"Stop or I'll shoot!" the cop ordered.

Tim let out a bestial growl as he took three quick steps toward the door. Officer Patterson shot Tim in the leg. He fell to the floor again and started to crawl then stood up.

"What the hell is wrong with you? Stay down," Officer Patterson shouted.

Tim shambled closer. Officer Patterson backed out of the doorway and ordered everyone else to do the same. Ana just stood there frozen and wide-eyed. Tim walked out of the room and turned his head towards Ana. Tim reached for Ana and managed to scratch her arm. Ana gasped and moved backwards. Tim tried to run at Ana as he dragged his hurt leg. Officer Patterson quickly stepped between Ana and Tim as he pushed Ana back. Officer Patterson ordered Tim to stop, but Tim swiped at him.

The officer then shot Tim twice in the chest. Tim kept reaching until a shot to the eye took him down for good. Tim's body slumped, unmoving, as the gore-splattered everywhere.

Everyone heard another scream from the room where Tonya was resting. They rushed to see who'd been hurt when they found the registrar backing out of from Tonya's room, where she planned to collect insurance information and hopefully a copay. The injured patient hurried into the hall. Her skin was pale, and her lips had gone blue. The irises of her eyes had gone a cloudy white.

"Get away from her," Ana shouted, but it was too late.

Tonya jumped into action, pouncing on the registrar, managing to bite around her left eye. The registrar screamed hysterically as blood poured down her face. Tonya swallowed her first bite and went back for more, but Officer Patterson shot her in the head, and she fell to the floor. The registrar passed out, from either pain or shock. She'd lost a chunk of flesh around her eye, as well as the eye itself.

The pool of blood flowed from the injury, down the side of the registrar's face, and pooled around her head.

Dee moved forward to check on her, but Officer Patterson stopped her. "Don't."

"I can't just stand here and not do anything. Krystal's been hurt," Dee said.

"This must be the plague they sent me down here to help with. This area is now quarantined, and whatever's going on, the Hazmat Team will need to evaluate her first."

The registrar sat up and trained her one remaining eye on Officer Patterson. Her skin was the same chalky pallor as the others. He lifted his weapon and aimed for her head.

"If you're still hearing me, stop right there. I *will* shoot you," he warned.

Her blue lips retracted in a grimace as she growled and got to her feet. Just as she lunged for him, the cop shot her in the forehead. She dropped to the floor and didn't move. He holstered his weapon and stumbled over to a chair next to Ana.

"I don't understand. They look dead and not reacting to pain?" he muttered, in shock at having shot three people in ten minutes.

He closed his eyes and ignored the nurse's mumbled reply. Everything sounded muffled to him anyway. He didn't have time to react when Ana's eyes opened to reveal white irises. She dove onto him, taking a bite out of his neck chewing quickly then severed his jugular as she went back for more. He bled out in seconds as Ana continued to his ear. Dee and Dr. Jacobs watched startled as they saw his skin go pale and jumped back in shock when he started moving.

Dr. Jacobs and Dee ran into his office and locked the door behind them. They cowered down out of sight.

"It's zombies!" Dee declared.

Dr. Jacobs shook his head. "Don't be silly. Zombies don't exist. There is a scientific explanation for what just happened. It's probably some kind of drug like PCP or bath salts."

Dee aimed a disbelieving look at him. "The cop who arrived perfectly fine fifteen minutes ago was on PCP? Come on, Brian.

Before he turned, did that same cop shoot a guy in the chest twice and that guy just kept coming?"

"Yeah," he reluctantly agreed.

"Zombies," she said firmly. "Did you see someone you knew who definitely died rise up again?" she asked, pointing at the not-so-friendly nurse on the other side of the door who just grabbed a security guard.

"Yes," he muttered.

"Zombies." She gestured to the door again. "And did you see them only stop after being shot in the head, permanently damaging the brain?"

He shook his head as if he was trapped in a bad dream and desperately tried to wake up. "This can't be real. Zombies aren't real."

Dee shrugged. "And yet they are eating people in our hospital right now. We have to get the hell out of here. The hospital is no place to be during a zombie apocalypse."

"Where do you suggest we go?" he asked, looking hopeless.

"Literally anywhere else. Do you have any medical supplies in here? Grab what you can. We'll have to break a window. There's no way I'm going back out there."

Dr. Jacobs stayed low as he went to his desk and grabbed his work bag and dumped everything on the floor. Dee started handing him some supplies she found in his office and saw his keys.

"The key to my car is in my locker. We'll have to take your Jeep."

Chapter Six

Phoenix, Arizona

Friday, May 11, 18:20

Terrence Bookman walked down the street, holding one hand to his stomach and the other to his head. He'd felt off since lunch, but that had just been one of those meal replacement shakes he'd had a hundred times before when he couldn't get away from his desk to eat. It felt like he was coming down with something serious. The pounding in his head was killing him, but he couldn't afford to be sick right now. Not with the merger still hanging in the balance. He'd just gotten back from a weekend in Colorado fishing with his brother. He had to hold it together. It was just the flu.

The weakness and exhaustion overwhelmed him, but he pushed on, just wanting to make it home and fall into bed. He passed a homeless man sitting on the sidewalk with his back up against a brick building.

"Hey, man. The name's Tom. I'm a wounded vet. You got any spare change?"

Terrence leaned against the building to catch his breath and patted his pockets. "I'm sorry. I only have my cards."

Tom laughed. "No problem, man. You can CashApp or PayPal me."

Terrence's hand went to his throat. It tightened and he struggled to breathe.

"Hey, you don't look too good, buddy," Tom said.

Terrence slumped against the wall, suddenly too tired to even stand. "I might need help," he slurred before passing out.

A group of teens passing by saw the unconscious businessman and rifled through his pockets. They took his valuables, even as Tom shouted to stop them. He'd been paralyzed on one side and couldn't muster the speed to do much physically. When they'd gotten what they wanted, the teens left Terrence alone. Tom pulled Terrence to a sitting position and shook him gently.

"Hey, man. Are you alright? I tried to stop them." Terrence's head fell forward and he slumped, not breathing. "Someone call an ambulance!"

He rolled Terrence onto his back and felt for a pulse. He found nothing and checked again. Still no pulse. He sat back and sighed. "I'm sorry, man."

Tom sat, lost in thoughts of what to do next, and did not notice when Terrance sat up. With his mouth open wide, Terrence sprang for the homeless man. Upon realizing he was in danger, Tom tried to move away, but the businessman grabbed the homeless man's shirt and pulled Tom closer and closer to his mouth. Finally, the businessman latched on to the homeless man's ear as the homeless man tried to jerk away at the last second. Terrence savagely bit off Tom's ear as he screamed.

Patrons of a nearby all-night gym filed outside to see what the commotion was all about. A guy in gym gear dropped his duffle bag and hurried over to help the screaming homeless man. Terrence took a chunk out of the gym patriot's leg for his troubles. Even through the pain, the fit man managed to pull his injured leg out of the businessman's mouth and kick him down on the ground.

The fit man then turned the businessman onto his stomach and held Terrence down with the knee of his good leg on Terrence's back.

"Somebody call the police!" he shouted.

"I called them," answered a woman in yoga pants as she approached. "They should be here in a few minutes."

More and more people gathered around the spectacle, pulling out their phones to record everything. Meanwhile, Terrence struggled like mad to get free. He growled and snapped at the gathered people, his white eyes seeing nothing but food.

"The cops better get here soon," the good Samaritan said as he fought to maintain control over Terrence, who thrashed underneath him with no signs of his energy waning. "This guy is acting like a wild animal."

One of the bystanders moved in closer to get a better angle of Terrence's eyes. No one expected the sudden lunge he made to bite the hand that filmed him. The budding cinematographer dropped his phone and cursed.

"Stay back everyone. He's attacking anyone he can reach," said the fit man on Terrence's back. "Where's that ambulance? Did anyone check on the guy he bit?"

Tom slumped to the ground, much to the surprise of those who'd been trying to stop the bleeding from his wound. The man holding Terrence down started to lose his strength; weakness overtook him. When everyone turned to look at Tom, Terrence managed to slip free and dove for one of the bystanders in the crowd, tearing into her leg. Tom stood as if he was a Marionette, and grabbed one of the men closest to him, biting deep into his bicep.

As the blood spilled, screams filled the night and people started to panic. Some froze, unable to move, while others didn't hesitate to shove anyone who happened to be between them and safety. The man who'd tried to help Tom rose from the ground, paled skinned and blue-lipped. He joined the others feasting on the crowd. Some people turned almost instantly; others took a few minutes. But everyone who was bitten or scratched turned eventually.

It spread quickly, with the first three people bitten by Terrence already turned and was eating others. The zombies were easily distracted and often abandoned fresh meals in search of those still trying to flee. Some of the bitten tried to make it home to clean their wounds. Some of them ran straight to the hospital or police station. Some of them turned right away and spread the infection further across the city with Terrence at the epicenter.

When the police finally arrived, the scene was pure chaos. Several bodies lay on the ground, their skulls smashed, and brains removed. Everywhere else, zombies chased those still living, with the living losing the battle over and over. The officers jumped out of their patrol car and went for Terrence, who was closest to them. The first officer drew his weapon and approached Terrance, who was currently dining on the intestines of an unfortunate gym patron. The second officer called for backup as they got closer to Terrence.

"Back away from the victim, now," the officer demanded.

Terrence didn't react. "He said move, punk. Stand up with your hands above your head," the second officer said.

Terrence turned his head towards the cops. He rose from his meal, then turned his full body towards the officers. His face and body were covered in blood and gore, which made his ghostly pale skin stand out even more.

"Get down on the ground," the first cop said, pointing his weapon at Terrence.

Terrence stumbled forward with his hands outstretched toward the officer. "Stop right where you are or I'll shoot," the officer warned.

Terrence, once he found his footing, started running at the police officers. Both officers opened fire, one aiming for the chest and the other for the abdomen. But Terrence kept coming. He charged forward and grabbed the first officer, managing to bite the man's forehead, the powerful jaws crunching into the bone. As his partner screamed in pain, the second officer pulled Terrence away and shoved him to the ground so hard, it caused the second police officer to stumble a little.

The second cop turned to shoot Terrence, but Terrence seamlessly sprang to his feet and tried to attack the 2nd officer. The second officer turned out of the way only narrowly missing a full-on tackle. Terrence lunged for his prey again, scratching the cop's hand before one of the wild shots hit Terrence in the head. He slumped unmoving to the ground as the sirens of backup sounded in the distance.

Once the extra officers arrived, they futility tried to detain and put down the remaining infected that was still in the area. Those who were hurt or turned into a zombie moved further and further away. Once it was deemed safe enough, paramedics arrived to help treat the wounded. The officer who was second on scene, had his wound cleaned and treated, but the officer who'd been bitten on the forehead was sent by ambulance to the closest hospital. The second officer filled his supervisor in on the situation and was sent back to the station to wait for the chief.

Fort Polk South, Louisiana

Friday, May 11, 18:10

Many of the military personnel stationed at the Louisiana base chose to spend their free time calling their loved ones back home. After finishing their duties for the day, a few wandered over to the game room to watch television. Carlos Jimenez found his battle buddy, Drew Adams sprawled out over one of the three coveted recliners with the remote in his hand. Jimenez snagged one of the recliners and sat beside him in front of the flat-screen television.

"What are we watching," he asked. "007? John Wick?"

"Fried Green Tomatoes," Adams answered without taking his attention from the screen.

Jimenez turned his head and stared at Adams for a bit. "I'm sorry, what did you say?"

Adams looked Jimenez in the eyes and spoke slowly. "Fried. Green. Tomatoes." He grinned and turned back to the screen. "Now shut up. I love this movie."

Jimenez shook his head but sat back to watch the movie. They were soon joined by Scott Peters, who took the last recliner. "Hey, are Thornton and Nguyen still off base?"

"Yep," Adams said.

Peters pulled out his phone to send a text. "Hopefully I can catch them, and they'll get me a Mexican pizza."

"How are you still hungry?" Jimenez asked.

"I should have gone with them when they left," Peters said. "But I changed my mind too late. I didn't eat much at dinner tonight. I just want a little something extra."

"It's possible they made a couple of stops before they got to Taco Bell. You might as well contact them," Adams said.

Peters whooped in delight when he received a text. "Nguyen said they'll grab me one. Man, that was great timing on my part." He sat back in the chair and looked up at the screen. "Sweet! I love this movie."

Jimenez grumbled, "Yeah, but we could be watching Die Hard or even Hot Fuzz."

Adams smiled. "Just give in, Jimenez. You can admit you like it, too."

Across the room, five soldiers sat by themselves at a table, unplayed cards dealt in front of them.

"I think we should go to the clinic, you guys," Angel said.

Riley shook his head. "I'd rather not."

"I don't want to go either," Bisley added. "We just need to drink more fluids and flush whatever this is out of our system."

"Maybe we overdid it in Colorado while on leave and just need more time to recover," King said.

"I'm not going to the clinic for an extended hangover to have that in my permanent record," Wolfe said, standing up. "But I don't want to hang out here anymore, either. I'm going back to my bunk to lie down. 'Night."

"Night," the other four chorused as they raised one hand in the air.

Angel stood up. "Simple or not, I don't feel right. I'm going over to the clinic to get checked out."

Bisley nodded knowingly. "Right. And I'm sure that cute nurse has nothing to do with it."

Angel grinned. "Well, she doesn't *not* have anything to do with it."

As Angel left, Riley winced as another sharp cramp shot through his stomach. "Ugh. I'm not feeling great either. I don't think the clinic can do anything for it though."

"I'll grab us some water," King said. He stood up slowly to accommodate the dizziness he felt, but still only made it two steps before he collapsed to the floor. As other soldiers rushed over to help, Riley and Bisley passed out, slumping unconscious over the table.

A few miles from the base, Thornton turned the corner, eating his burrito as Nguyen unwrapped a taco in the passenger seat. Nguyen heard his phone chime and wiped his hands to check the message. If there were any more last-minute orders, they were too late. He read the text, staring at it in shock.

"What is it?" Thornton asked. "Peters decide he needs more than a Mexican pizza?"

"It's from Peters," Nguyen said. "It says 'DON'T COME BACK! ZOMBIES!' Like, what am I supposed to do what that information? We can't *not* go back. And zombies? Come on, that's not even a good prank."

"I'm getting really bad vibes," Thornton said. "He's probably just messing with us, but I saw some weird stuff on the news about Louisiana, Colorado and several other states this evening before we left."

On base, a soldier name Private Leo Thompson ran into the armory. "I need guns and a lot of ammo, right now!" he said frantically.

"Paperwork?" the bored quartermaster asked.

"Listen to the screams, man! There are people out there eating people!" Thompson shouted, anxious to have some firepower; some way to protect himself from the hell on Earth the base had become. "And that's not all. I know it sounds insane, but it's full-on zombies out there, man. We need guns and ammo if any of us are going to survive the night."

"Whatever happened, you need to file a report of the incident with your Commanding Officer, or go to an MP directly," the quartermaster answered, looking at Thompson over his glasses.

"You cannot be serious right now. Well, if there are rabid people out there taking down other people twice their size. I'm going to need something other than brute strength to survive. I'm going to need guns." Thompson said.

"You should know the rules, Private. Besides, the way you're talking, I don't think you need a gun, you need to go see a medic."

"Just know I warned you." Thompson said letting out a loud sigh then ran outside seeing a few zombies in the distance feast upon their screaming meals.

If he wanted to survive, Thompson needed to get off the base. Right now. Thompson moved strategically, using the ample cover of vehicles and equipment to stay out of sight. He tried to block out the screams of suffering he heard. Those were his friends. His brothers. And now they were soulless monsters who wanted to eat him.

The speed of the axis-shifting changes was too hard to process, so he went into survival mode. He couldn't stop to look. He couldn't stop to help. He was on his own.

Thompson made it to the front of the base after what felt like an eternity to the traumatized soldier. Now, he just needed to make it to the road. Thompson saw the headlights of an approaching car and waved at it. The headlights shut off and the car remained idling. Thompson ran for the car with everything he had left.

In the car, Thornton and Nguyen cautiously watched the base, they started driving slowly toward the front gates.

"Is that someone running towards us?" asked Thornton squinting.

"I've been calling and texting Adams. There's no reply from him. I can't get anyone on base to answer. Not even the main base number or the guard shack. Those phones are staffed twenty-four hours a day. Something's wrong."

"There's definitely something going on. I can hear gunfire in the distance. And screaming," Thornton said. "Is that a group of people chasing that person?"

"Oh my God, stop the car!" Nguyen yelled. "Stop!"

Thornton slammed on the brakes. "What's wrong?"

Nguyen pointed to the guard shack, where they could clearly see one guard eating another, and further in, they could see some soldiers eating other soldiers.

"This can't be real," Thornton said as he rubbed his temples. A Drill? No, no one's wearing their PT belt."

"Look over there," Nguyen pointed, "It doesn't look like that guy's gonna make it."

Thornton gulped down a deep breath. "This has to be some kind of sick joke." He hit the gas as he turned the wheel towards the sprinting figure. The car shot forward toward Thompson.

"The military doesn't have a sense of humor, Thornton. This must be real," Nguyen said.

The car jumped the curb and did a slick U-turn around Thompson before sliding to a stop. Thornton unlocked the doors and Thompson jumped in, slamming the door shut behind him.

"Drive!" Thompson shouted.

"Obviously," Thornton said, stomping on the gas pedal and throwing up clumps of grass as the tires spun for a moment before catching. The car sped away and the zombie soldiers worked their way out into the streets in search of food.

"What the hell is going on?" Thornton yelled as they got further away from the base.

"I don't know how to explain it," Thompson said. He sat panting in the back seat, simply relieved to be alive and not one of those things. "It was just like in the zombie movies, man. People were biting and eating people. Then they'd turn into one of those white-eyed freaks and start trying to eat anyone they could reach. They turned so fast."

"Was everyone a zombie?" Nguyen asked, horrified.

Thompson shook his head. "I don't know. It was chaos. People were running everywhere. There was so much blood. I didn't know who was themselves and who was a zombie."

Nguyen shook his head and buried his face in his hands.

Thornton stayed quiet as he drove toward Texas, hoping to find help across the state line.

Part Three: Overcome

Chapter Seven

Aurora, Colorado

Saturday, May 12, 07:57

Chuck woke up early to make breakfast for everyone. They all ate and gathered in the living room to watch the news; certain they would see the results of their actions recognized by the world. Every news channel was ablaze with reports of a mysterious unknown disease epidemic that had broken out in several cities across America, with new reports coming in constantly.

"Investigators believe this is possibly a new strain of flu. They urge everyone to use stringent sanitation measures and to get the available flu shot," one reporter said.

Dale laughed. "A flu shot isn't going to do much to protect from this."

A broad grin spread across Victor's face. "It's begun."

"I thought we might get a few dozen," Chuck said, stunned. He let out a wicked laugh. "It sounds like there are hundreds already and more every day."

"How do we let everyone know it was us and why we did it?" Bernie asked.

"Well, let's not make it too easy on the police. Wouldn't want them to think we had to do their job for them," Dale said. "Let them put in the work to figure it out."

"Exactly," Victor said, his eyes wide as he tried to take in all the scenes of destruction they'd caused.

They all stayed to watch the news for a while, but eventually, Victor, Dale, and Chuck wandered off to do other things. Bernie stayed in the living room, his attention glued to the television and the reports coming in from around the country and several places around the world. He felt growing conflict about what they'd done. It sounded like the effects were a lot worse than they'd imagined. Then he saw another breaking news report.

"The latest reports indicate that victims of this mysterious disease can be identified by their chalky pale skin, blue lips, and white irises. Those with the disease have become violent and aggressive. In all cases so far, they will attack and attempt to eat anyone they can reach. Viewers, this is not a hoax. This information has been confirmed to be true. Those affected by the disease do not die unless catastrophic damage is done to the brain. They will get up from mortal wounds and continue attacking. Everyone is advised to secure yourselves in your homes and not approach these infected individuals for any reason. Stay safe and let the authorities deal with this matter," a national news reporter said.

Bernie jumped up and ran to the kitchen, where the others had gathered. "You guys, I think we might have messed up. I've been watching the news, and the people who drank the water are turning into zombies. They are eating people! And then turning them into zombies."

All three of the other men jumped up and followed Bernie back to the living room to watch the news reports. Every channel was variations on the same thing. The world was in the grips of a zombie outbreak.

"We need to get further away from Colorado," Victor urged. "Yesterday."

"Yeah, this whole area is a hot zone. The further away from Colorado we are, the better," Chuck said.

"What about Texas?" Bernie asked. "I know there might be some outbreaks there, too, but there will be plenty of people with guns, they have their own water source, and, best of all, they have their own source of agriculture."

"I can't think of a better plan right now," Victor said, standing. "Get your go bags packed and be ready to go in an hour. I want to get out before all hell breaks loose."

"Right now?" Dale asked as he stood up. "Wendy is still at work. We need to wait for her."

Victor pointed to the television, which showed graphic scenes of the carnage the zombies left in their wake. "Does that look like we have time for her to finish her shift? We can't stay, Dale. If this is moving as fast as the news says it is, we have to go now or we won't make it out alive."

"I can't leave her behind," Dale said. "She's family. And she took us in. Please, Victor. I'm not leaving without her."

"No, Dale." Chuck said as he stood. "I love you like an uncle, but we cannot stay all day. Things are going to get real bad real quick. What we need to do is make sure we're not here when that happens."

Dale stared at Victor intently, shaking his head.

"But, Da-," Chuck tried to protest.

"Vic, we nee-," Dale tried to plead.

"Enough of this!" Victor roared as he threw up his hands. "Chuck, we need to pack. We need food and water to survive, and we're going to give Wendy an hour to get here. And Dale, grow up. Our lives depend on what we do in the next hour." Victor started rubbing his eyes. "Dale, call Wendy back here, now! I respect Wendy and I'm grateful, but we need to leave in an hour with or without her."

Dale looked like he'd been slapped, but he hurried to call Wendy and make her come back.

Victor turned to Bernie and tossed him the keys. "Take my vehicle to the grocery store down the road. Use Wendy's credit card she left for emergencies and get all the nonperishable food and water you can get."

"You want me to drive into town in that?" Bernie asked, puzzled. "I thought we were keeping the SUV out of sight."

Victor shot Bernie an annoyed look. "Clearly the situation has changed. We've already gone through a lot of the water we had for bathing, eating, and cleaning. We need water and food if we're going to make it to Texas."

Bernie shrugged. "Well, hopefully, everyone else doesn't have the same idea. When there's a hint of snow, people always swarm the stores. What do you think zombies will do?"

While Bernie was gone, the other three worked fast to get all their things packed and ready to be loaded into the SUV. Bernie returned forty minutes later, with the back of the vehicle mostly full of water and groceries from the store, leaving just enough room for their gear.

Bernie backed into the garage and closed the door. Minutes later, the guys were loading their gear into the SUV.

"I got plenty of food and water, and filled the Equinox up with gas, too." Bernie said once they finished loading the SUV. The four walked back into the house and headed for the living room. "Surprisingly, the store was almost empty. How much longer until Wendy gets here?"

"She should be here any minute," Dale said as he walked over to the window and started looking out for any sign of her.

Five minutes later, Wendy pulled into the driveway and hurried into the house. "Dale, what in the world is going on?"

"Good, you're here," Chuck said. "Let's go."

"Wait for just a second," Wendy demanded. "Someone better tell me what's going on or I'm not going anywhere."

Dale took her by the arm. "Things are going from bad to worse," he said.

"People aren't dying like we thought they would. Well, they *are* dying, but they're coming back as zombies. We need to get out of Colorado. We think Texas is the best idea."

Wendy stood silently for a moment, staring at Dale in confusion. "What!" she yelled. "You said it was an emergency! Did I leave my job for *this*? Zombies aren't real, Dale."

"He's not lying," Bernie said. "Haven't you seen the news? We should have left already, but we waited for you."

Wendy's brows furrowed. "I don't believe this. I don't know what you're playing at, but I left work early for your *emergency,*" Wendy said while doing air quotes in the air. "I won't get paid for those hours."

Dale took her arm again, but she pulled it out of his grasp. He folded his hands into a praying motion and looked into her eyes. "Wendy, please. This is not a game or some kind of joke. It was the drugs we dumped in the water. They aren't killing people; they're turning people into *zombies.*"

"That's it. You four have outstayed your welcome," Wendy said coldly. "Get out of my house. Now!"

Wendy turned and started heading towards her bedroom.

Dale went after her, grabbed her by the arm, and pulled her to the living room where the graphic news reports still played on a loop. "It's on every channel," Dale said, "This is real, and it's spreading fast. We need to get out of here."

She stood in stunned shock as she tried to take in the news reports. It truly was on every channel. "I don't know what to believe. This can't be happening."

"Believe me, Wendy," Dale pleaded. "Pack your stuff. You have five minutes."

Wendy gave in and hurried to her room to pack the essentials. While she packed, the guys made sure their clips where full with one in the chamber. They also made sure their backup magazines were full.

"I've got everything packed, but it will be too tight if we all go in your SUV, Victor." Wendy said while walking towards the front door. "I'm going to take my car. Dale, ride with me, but grab the little bit of food and water I have in the pantry and help me load it in my trunk.

"We've already got it loaded," Dale said, pushing Wendy toward the door. "Yeah, I'll ride with you. Let's just go,"

Wendy stashed her two suitcases in her trunk and opened the passenger door to toss her jacket into the front seat. Dale pulled a case of water from Victor's SUV and turned to take it to Wendy's car. He'd only made it about halfway when Wendy's neighbor ran from the other side of her house and grabbed her. The neighbor proceeded to try and bite her.

"No!" Dale screamed, who ran and then threw the case of water at the zombie, breaking its grip on her.

Victor, who was at the back of his SUV trying to arrange the last few items, ran to the opening of the garage trying to find out why Dale was yelling. Once there, he saw Dale trying to pull a zombie off Wendy. "Boys, get your guns ready!" Victor yelled as he ran over to help Dale and Wendy.

Chuck and Bernie stepped out of the garage, guns at the ready. Wendy broke away from her neighbor and fell to the ground. She scrambled back as Dale and Victor fought with the zombie.

The man was completely rabid. He kept trying to bite Dale on the face while Victor stood behind the neighbor pulling on its neck with his arm. It took all their considerable strength to stop the neighbor. The commotion and their shouting caught the attention of several neighbors, who'd also been turned. Chuck and Bernie started taking shots and gaped in shock when a zombie took a shot to the chest and kept coming. Chuck made a shot between the zombie's eyes, and it fell, unmoving.

"The head!" Chuck shouted over the gunshots. "Aim for the head!"

With well-placed headshots, they quickly executed the approaching zombies, but couldn't get a good shot on the one Victor and Dale fought. Chuck only managed to hit Wendy's car.

Bernie jumped up on the porch to keep watch for more zombies while Chuck rushed forward to help the others. With his arm hooked around the zombie's throat, Victor pulled back as hard as he could, leaving the zombie exposed to Chuck's shot. Chuck put his gun against the zombie's temple and pulled the trigger.

Wendy screamed. Blood splattered her face and she looked horrified. "I think some of the blood got in my mouth!" She retched into the grass.

"Are you alright?" Chuck asked, offering her a hand.

She shook her head. "Of course not. My neighbor, J-Jason, just tried t-to eat me." She stammered in shock. "He's a zombie. Jason is a zombie and he tried to eat me. We gotta get out of here. Right now."

"That's what we've been saying, Wendy. Your car got hit in the fight. I can see its leaking antifreeze," Bernie said. "You'll have to squeeze in the SUV with us."

They had Wendy's stuff stashed in the Equinox in less than a minute. "Can you grab a wet towel before we leave, Dale? I need to wash this blood off my face."

Bernie groaned. "Hurry. We need to go!"

"I'll be fast. Start the SUV. I'll be back in a minute." Dale ran into the house and true to his word, returned in less than a minute.

Victor hopped in the driver's seat while Chuck helped Wendy into the back middle seat, then got in behind his dad. Bernie jumped into the back passenger seat. Once Dale returned, he hurried into the front passenger seat. Wendy took the towel gratefully, using it to wipe the blood from her skin. Victor hit the gas before they'd all buckled their seatbelts.

"Take Buckley to Quincy. We'll want to take as many back roads as we can," Dale said. "Let's avoid the highways. They'll be clogged and the zombies will be attracted to large groups of people."

Victor nodded. "That's the plan. That atlas should help us make it there. Is anyone hurt?"

"No. It all happened so quickly. He appeared from out of nowhere and just grabbed her," Dale said.

"It would have been so much worse if you hadn't stopped him. Thank you. Thank all of you. You saved my life," Wendy said.

Bernie cleared his throat. "I hate to be the one to say this, but if zombie movies have taught us anything, cross contamination of zombie fluids in any way can make you turn. We need to watch her."

Dale glared at him. "Shut up, Bernie! She isn't going to turn into a zombie. This isn't a movie. This is real life."

Bernie glared right back, pointing out the window. "And those are real zombies out there. Eating real people. I'm sure everything won't be the same as the movies, they're not slow with rigor mortis for one. Or should we be calling them infected since they move at regular speed. Either way, I'm just saying, we need to watch Wendy. To be prepared when she turns."

"She isn't going to turn!" Dale shouted.

"Stop talking about me like I'm not here!" Wendy spoke up. "I'm not hurt. I didn't get bitten or scratched. I just got some blood on me. I *feel* fine. I'll *be* fine."

Bernie caught Chuck's gaze. Chuck nodded. Wendy looked back and forth between them.

"I saw that," she said.

"Keep a sharp eye out, in all directions," Victor said. "Things are going to get a lot worse before we get to Texas."

Wendy rubbed her eyes and Bernie stared at her in disgust. He could still see flecks of blood on her fingers. She leaned back against the seat and closed her eyes, suddenly exhausted with all of this. Wendy fell into a fitful sleep and stayed that way for nearly ten minutes. Victor swerved to avoid a zombie on the road. Wendy's head fell to the side and her eyes opened. She lunged for Bernie's neck.

He'd been on alert for this exact thing and hit her with an elbow to the jaw. "Someone get her!" he shouted.

He held Wendy's right wrist with his left hand and jammed his right elbow under her chin, forcing her face toward the roof. Chuck grabbed Wendy's left wrist and held it down as she growled and snarled, struggling to get free.

"Wendy! What are you doing? Stop it!" Dale said, turning around in his seat.

"Stop the SUV, Dad!" Chuck screamed. "She's turned."

Victor immediately turned off of Buckley Road onto East Nassau Drive. He jumped out and ripped the back door open. Victor pulled Chuck out of the cab. Wendy, who'd been in the middle, lunged out after him. Bernie quickly let go of Wendy and slipped out the door, closing it behind him.

"She's not a zombie," Dale muttered. "She can't be."

Victor wrestled Wendy to the ground and held her there with a knee in the middle of her back. Dale scrambled out of the front seat to join them.

"What are you going to do?" Dale asked. "Let's just talk about this."

Chuck cocked his pistol and aimed it at Wendy's temple.

"No, wait!" Dale said, holding his hand up for Chuck to stop.

Chuck hesitated and looked up at Dale, but Bernie unholstered his gun and shot Wendy between the eyes in one smooth motion. The others stared at him in stunned silence.

"She was a zombie, you guys," Bernie said, agitated as he holstered his gun. "If we hesitate, we all die."

Dale glared at him in disbelief. "But she was my family!"

"She was a zombie!" Bernie said firmly. "She wasn't human anymore."

Dale grabbed him by the collar, spun Bernie around, and slammed him into the side of the SUV. "You shut your mouth!"

Chuck tried to pull Dale off of Bernie, but Dale pushed Chuck to the ground. Victor split them apart and held them both at arm's length. "I know you're hurting, Dale. And I know Bernie has a smart mouth and not enough sense to know when to keep it shut, but you need to breathe and think. Wendy turned into a zombie. I'm sorry for that, brother, but we need to protect ourselves."

Dale glared at Bernie but didn't say a word. Bernie stared back, utterly unapologetic. Dale pulled Wendy's body out of the street and onto the grass while Victor pulled Wendy's suitcases out of the trunk and left them next to her body. Dale walked around the vehicle and got in the front passenger seat, dazed, and shaking his head as if he couldn't believe the last few minutes. The others got into the SUV.

Bernie tossed the bloodstained towel into the road and doused his hands with sanitizer.

Bernie kept his hard expression, but his hands shook as he buckled his seatbelt. He glanced around at the others, but no one seemed to have seen him. He shoved his hands between his legs until they stopped shaking. Victor put his SUV in gear, hit a U-turn, and started back on their route.

Occasionally, they heard screams as they drove, watching people fleeing by foot and by car. Cars blew through red lights, causing accidents. Zombies pounced on their victims, pulling them from the broken cars and devouring their screaming meals. The mangled victims would then rise as zombies and set out to find victims of their own.

Victor dove as safely as he could, but he had to slow down to work his way through a minefield of obstacles. Bernie caught sight of a zombie in jogging clothes who'd spotted them in the SUV and turned to run toward them.

"Oh, man! That zombie is running straight for us. Victor, drive faster!" Bernie cried.

"I'm trying not to hit or get hit by anything," Victor snapped. "You can see this, right?"

The jogger caught up to them and started banging on the back passenger window, trying to get to Chuck. He slammed his hands and head into the glass over and over, growling snarling. Chuck rolled down the window and the zombie outreached its arms for Chuck. Chuck was ready. With his gun already drawn, Chuck shot the zombie between the eyes. The limp weight caused the now truly deceased zombie to tumble to the ground.

Victor hit the brakes hard and swerved to the right, narrowly missing the front end of a Buick Sedan that had crossed the median. A woman carrying an infant ran into the street, waving at the men with her free arm.

"Help me!" she screamed.

Victor swerved again and narrowly missed the mother.

"We should help her," Bernie urged. "She has a baby!"

Victor shook his head. We can't help every person we see along the way.

We only have so much room, food, water, and bullets."

"I know that. Not all of them. Just her," Bernie insisted.

"Oh, you want to help the pretty lady with a baby, Bernie. Is that because you feel guilty after murdering Wendy?" Dale snarled.

A zombie stumbled around a crashed car and came after the mother. The mother screamed and ran after Victor's vehicle, still calling for help. She wasn't fast enough to escape her fate, though. The zombie grabbed the mother, biting her between the shoulder blades. She nearly dropped her baby and Bernie watched in horror. Another zombie ran up and started gnawing on her free arm. When a third zombie sprinted up and snatched the baby, she had no way to stop it.

The mother screamed in agony as she watched her baby's flesh tourn by the teeth of a monster, but her torment did not last long. She turned quickly, rising as a zombie in search of prey of her own.

"That's so messed up," Bernie said, eyes wide. "Victor, a zombie just ate that baby. We could have saved them both!"

"We can't save everyone," Victor repeated. "I'm sure we'll come across plenty more people in need along the way. We can't save ourselves if we try to save everyone else."

Bernie looked at Victor in disbelief, then back at the spot where the horrifying event took place. A clueless man walked down the street wearing earbuds. He never saw the zombie who ripped out his throat. They passed a driver with his arm hanging out the window. He made an easy meal for a passing zombie. The driver yanked his arm back, and hit the gas, crashing into another vehicle.

Victor drove on and eventually turned left onto Quincy, disregarding the red light and ignoring the few random honks from the cars that chose to stop. He passed a sporting goods store and then a gas station. Both seemed to be operating as usual while the chaos moved ever closer. People were going about their typical day, not even aware of the nightmare that was sweeping through the city toward them.

Chuck shook his head as they passed a Starbucks with a long drive-through line. They had no idea of the danger that were mere blocks away.

As the number of zombies increased, traffic got thicker. Drivers swerved and laid into their horn anytime someone blocked their way or wasn't moving fast enough. Victor pulled off onto the grass and hit the gas pedal. He moved around the slower vehicles and forced his way back into traffic as they moved under the bridge.

"Get ready, fellas," Victor said. "We've got zombies coming right at us."

The men readied their weapons. A zombie pulled ahead of the pack and Bernie rolled down his window to aim. He missed with his first shot, but the second hit the zombie's shoulder. A third shot hit right between the eyes and brought the zombie down hard. Victor swerved again and Chuck grabbed his friend to keep him from falling.

They shot any zombie who got too close as Victor worked the SUV out of the close quarters. They saw people get eaten and rise as zombies. Someone who saw Victor's SUV, moving through the destruction, ran toward them, yelling desperately and waving his arms.

"Help me, please!"

"Aww, did you hear that?" Dale said, smirking cruelly. "That one said *please.*"

Victor chuckled and kept driving. Bernie sat in the back and watched them both with an incredulous look.

Chapter Eight

Aurora, Colorado

Saturday, May 12, 13:17

Along the way, they saw countless people dead and dying, with people many reanimating as zombies. Cars crashed constantly around them, with some occupants abandoning their cars to flee from the zombies suddenly riding with them.

Bernie sat wide-eyed and in shock as the miles continued. "We did this. These people are dying because of us."

"That *was* the plan, boy," Victor said sharply from the driver's seat. "People were always supposed to die. The only difference is, no one was supposed to come back as a zombie and try to eat *us*."

Chuck reached over and put a comforting hand on Bernie's shoulder. "Don't get weak on us now, Bern. We need you."

"I don't regret the plan to kill people," Bernie said. "We had to do *something*. I just wish people weren't dying like this. It's just horrible."

Victor shrugged. "Regardless of how they're doing it, people are dying."

"But they aren't *dying*," Bernie insisted, shaking his head. "They are turning and coming back as zombies hell-bent on making more zombies. Now our lives are in danger, too. Our entire way of life is going to change."

"Once we reach Texas, everything will be alright," Chuck said.

Dale rolled his eyes at Chuck's efforts to comfort his friend.

"Victor, turn right onto Kiowa-Bennett Road," Dale said. "It should be coming up."

Victor stopped at the stop sign. After a car passed, he crossed the intersection.

"Hey, that was Kiowa Road," Chuck said. "You just passed it."

Victor pulled over and looked back at the sign.

"No, that says CR137," Victor said.

"Yeah, but in small letters, it reads Kiowa-Bennett Road," Chuck replied.

"Yeah, it's small, but it says Kiowa-Bennett Road in the top right," Bernie said turned in his seat squinting, then pointing.

"Okay," Victor said with a long, drawn-out sigh. "Not sure why they would have two names on the sign and make the second one so small."

After a truck passed, Victor made a U-turn, stopped at the stop sign, and then turned left onto Kiowa-Bennett Road/CR137.

Okay, keep straight, turn right when this road ends, and then make an immediate left," Dale said as he looked over the map. We'll take that down to 86."

Victor followed Dale's instructions. Bernie watched the landscape through the window. "There's a lot of nothing out here, except for trailer parks. So, cliché."

"That's what we want. The more of nothing there is, the fewer people and traffic we gotta deal with," Victor answered.

Victor drove on until he eventually got to a stop sign.

"Turn left here onto 86," Dale said, consulting the map again. "If we stay on this road, it will take us straight to Highway 70, and from there to Highway 287. We'll be in Texas in no time."

"Chuck, can you pass me some snacks?" Dale asked. I need something in my belly."

"Yeah, me too," Victor added.

Chuck passed around food and drinks and the group munched as they continued their journey. They traveled by fields, farms, and occasionally other motorists, but for the most part, the open highway was empty. They spotted one group on the side of the road who was stretching and walking around. The guys watched as another group of motorists stopped on the side of the road had the hood of their vehicle raised. Another group along the highway waved their arms for attention and cried for help. Some stranded motorists flipped them off as they drove by. Bernie had to look away when they passed an elementary school where zombies chased the few surviving students.

"Can you imagine what it'll be like when their parents go to pick them up?" Victor asked.

Bernie shook his head to clear the mental images of that very thing. "How do you think it spread this far? We're not even close to the Colorado River."

"It only takes one infected person to spread the disease and turn an entire town into zombies," Chuck said. "Someone here must have been to the Colorado River recently. They contracted the disease somehow, came back, and now this whole town and probably the next will end up as zombies. You saw how quickly Wendy turned. It only takes one."

Bernie thought of all the horror and destruction they'd caused. He couldn't see any message in that. Just death. "Did we do the right thing, guys?"

Everyone grew quiet and avoided eye contact. None of them wanted to admit their choice had likely brought about the end of the world. They'd only wanted to send a message, not start the apocalypse.

"*WE* made a choice and we're sticking by it," Victor said. He looked down at the fuel gauge.

"We're half empty. Check the map and see if there's anything close by. I'd like to top off while we still have the chance."

Dale nodded and checked the map for any small towns where they could hopefully get in and out of quickly. "Let's see. Lamar looks like a good choice. Big enough to have a gas station, small enough that it's probably empty of zombies. Let's stop there. Afterwards." Dale paused while looking at the map then continued, "Looks like once we get back on the road, you should take Hwy 287 around Boise City. Let's avoid areas we know will be populated."

Victor followed Dale's directions and they soon found themselves driving into Lamar, Colorado. A little ways into town, they spotted a Conoco. Victor pulled in, shutting the vehicle off next to the pumps.

"We should be okay once we reach Texas," Dale said. "I think it would be a good idea to get as much fuel as we can, though. Even if Texas has its own oil fields. It would be best not to stop too much, and we will need something to trade when we get there."

"Not a bad idea," Victor said. "Let's do it."

They all climbed out of the SUV and stretched their legs. Victor pumped the gas while Dale went inside and grabbed two large gas cans. Together, the two filled the cans and stashed them in the back of the SUV. Bernie went in to search the restroom while Chuck browsed the convenience store for any snacks he wanted. When they finished with the gas cans, Victor stayed with his SUV while Dale went to retrieve the boys. When they returned, they saw Victor with his hands in the air and a family pointing their guns at him.

The father was pointing a shotgun at Victor's head while the mother pointed a 9mm at Victor's chest. The son, who looked all of about twelve, also pointed a 9mm while the daughter, who looked around six, hugged her teddy bear. Chuck, Dale, and Bernie approached quietly, drawing their weapons.

"We only want your vehicle and supplies," the father said, his voice shaky. "We don't want to harm you, but we will. Just walk away and no one has to get hurt."

Dale cocked his pistol and stepped from behind the SUV. "That's not how this plays out, friend. Just put your guns down and walk away. I kinda don't want to hurt you."

"Are you actually willing to shoot kids?" the father asked, incredulous.

Chuck shifted his aim to the mom. "I'm willing to shoot anyone who threatens my dad."

The man wavered but he knew they needed the vehicle if they were going to survive. They couldn't stay in Colorado anymore. His resolve hardened. "Look, we don't need to turn this into a blood bath. Just give us what we want."

Victor shook his head and stood with his back straight at his full height. He was an imposing figure, leeching menace into the air around him. "Looks like we have ourselves a standoff here. You asked us if we would actually shoot kids. I think the real question is, are you actually willing to watch your kids die?"

The man cocked his gun in response, his family doing the same. He fixed his gun sight on Victor once more.

The mother aimed her gun between Dale and Chuck, ready to react if either of them moved. The son covered Bernie with his weapon.

Victor kept his voice calm and reasonable. "You can't cover all of us. We don't hold grudges. Just walk away now and no one gets hurt."

"We *need* those supplies and that SUV," the father insisted.

The little girl spotted a few zombies emerging from the Quality Inn across the street and screamed. "Mommy, monsters!"

Zombies came from the hotel chasing anyone nearby. Victor watched the spectacle from the corner of his eye as the zombies found any unlucky human. The screams permeated the area.

"You're wasting time. Time you need to get your family to safety," Victor said. "What's your next move? There are other vehicles. You only have one family."

"Please," the man pleaded. "I just need to take care of my family."

Victor shrugged. "Me too, brother. Yet we find ourselves in this here standoff. What makes your family more important than mine? Once again, your move. Time is running out." He gestured at the zombies.

Both parents turned their heads toward a scream, taking their attention off their quarry, to see someone pedaling furiously down the street and a kid running from a zombie, then, quickly turned their attention to where their little girl was standing. Relief washed over them.

While they were distracted, Victor seized the opportunity and lunged forward, snatching the father's gun and pulling it from his hand. Seeing her husband disarmed, the mother aimed her gun at Victor. Dale didn't hesitate and pulled the trigger, shooting the woman in the thigh but intentionally missing the major blood vessels. She fell to the ground, screaming.

"Mom!" the boy shouted, taking a shot at Dale and missed. The recoil was too much for his inept training. The boy dropped the gun while stumbling back.

Victor hadn't expected the boy to shoot. He stepped to the side but tripped on the gas station pavement and fell to the ground with a curse.

"Dad!" Chuck yelled.

Chuck pointed his gun at the boy. The father looked like he was about to dive for the mother's gun, but Dale trained his sights on the man's forehead.

"Don't make a bad situation even worse," Dale advised. "Kick the gun over here, pal. You too, young man. Slide your gun over." He turned back to the father. "And shame on you for not giving your boy proper training. You're going to get your family killed through sheer stupidity."

The father and son saw no other choice and slid over their weapons. The son looked to his father.

"No need to look at your dad, son," Dale said. "He can't help you in this situation."

Chuck bent over to pick up the new guns. Just then, the little girl pulled out a pocket pistol from her teddy bear and pointed it at Chuck's head.

"Honey, no!" the father screamed, extending a hand toward his daughter.

A gunshot broke the quiet of the night and the little girl's body fell to the ground. Everyone turned to look at Bernie, who held a pistol with smoke still curling from the barrel.

"Noooo!" the mother screamed. "You monster! You shot my little girl.

"Welp, it seems to me like you should have walked away when we gave you the chance," Victor said, shrugging as if he didn't have a care in the world. "Let's get out of here, fellas."

"You can't just leave us here like this after you shot my little girl," the father said, his voice sounding so lost and broken.

"Why not?" Victor asked coldly. "She's dead from your bad choices."

Chuck and Dale unloaded the new guns they collected, so they wouldn't misfire while they were on the road, then stashed the weapons in the trunk. Afterwards, they took their seats on the passenger side.

Victor, who had his gun aimed at the remaining family members, turned towards the SUV once he felt the family was no longer a threat and everyone was ready to go. Victor saw Bernie, standing frozen and wide-eyed, staring at the pistol in his hand.

Victor patted him on the back. "Come on, Bernie. Get in. You did good, son. I'm proud of you."

As they were about to start driving, the clerk, seemingly from the uniform, came out of the convenient store holding a handgun in his shaking hands. Chuck and Dale didn't hesitate. Both aimed their guns out their windows, centered directly on the clerk.

"Not today," Dale called out to him. "Not. Today."

The clerk pointed his gun at the ground and lifted his free hand into the air. Victor ignored him and pulled out onto the road, heading toward Texas. Bernie turned back to watch as the zombies from the hotel start crossing the street towards the distraught family. The father helped his wife up, but she fell to the ground, unable to support her weight on the injured leg. Her screams brought more zombies.

"Come on," the man urged his wife. "Let's go!"

But the wife could not run. She couldn't even stand. The man looked back and forth between his wife and his son. Recognizing the dilemma, he took the boy's hand and turned to run.

"Wait!" the wife screamed. Five zombies descended on her and began eating while two ignored the easy prey and went after the father and son. The gas station clerk raised his handgun and tried to help the woman.

"Get off her, you thugs," the clerk ordered. "Get off her, I said!"

A zombie turned away from the wife, who'd stopped screaming, and grabbed the clerk to take a bite from his arm. It didn't take long for the other zombies in the area to be drawn to the screams. Then the wife sat up with blue lips and white eyes to join the feast.

The father and son made it about fifty feet before a zombie grabbed the boy as they got to the Hickory House restaurant.

"Dad! Help me!" the boy screamed.

The father lost his grip on the boy's hand and turned to see a zombie pulling the boys arm to its mouth. A second zombie grabbed his head, its slavering lips still dripping blood from former victims. The boy struggled to get away, but his tiny body wasn't strong enough. The father's eyes went wide and filled with tears. There was nothing he could do. His entire family was gone in a matter of minutes. The man turned to run away.

"No, please!" the boy cried out. "Help me, Daddy. Don't leave me!"

Those were the boy's last words as he watched his father run away, leaving him to the monsters.

Chapter Nine

Lamar, Colorado
Saturday, May 12, 16:40

Inside the SUV, the men continued their journey. Bernie stared out the window without seeing anything. He hadn't spoken since shooting the child. Chuck thought he looked shell-shocked and slapped a hand on his back.

"You saved my life back there, Bern," Chuck said, gratitude in his voice.

Bernie shook his head slowly and his brows furrowed. "I shot and killed a little girl."

"A little girl who would have killed my son— your best friend— if you hadn't shot first," Victor corrected. "Think about it like that. You did good, Bernie. Her father should never have tried to steal my SUV and our gear. They would have left us for dead without a second thought. Her dad is the reason that whole event even happened."

Bernie sat there in a daze, only half listening to them drone on about how he'd done the right thing.

He nodded when they looked at him expectantly, but he didn't say a word. Bernie just sat there with a blank expression on his face. He couldn't get the image of the shocked "O" the mother's mouth had made when the bullet hit the little girl's chest. It was seared onto his brain, and he saw it every time he closed his eyes.

They drove on, weaving in and out of traffic on the two-lane highway before they had to slow down for a pair of trucks driving under the speed limit. Victor edged over to the left to get a peek around the truck in front of him. Nothing came toward them in the oncoming lane. He shifted to the oncoming lane and sped up to pass the truck. From this vantage, he could see an open space in the line of cars ahead of them. It seemed they weren't the only ones who were heading to Texas.

As Victor sped up to get ahead of the slow-moving traffic, a Subaru saw Victor trying to pass in its left side mirror and must have thought it was a good idea, because the driver swerved into the oncoming lane in front of Victor without warning, forcing Victor to hit his breaks. Victor honked the horn and gestured to the idiot driver.

"You're supposed to speed up when you pass someone, moron!" Victor shouted.

Victor stayed on the Subaru's bumper, hoping the driver would finally speed up and let them move forward. The oncoming lane wouldn't stay clear forever. Victor honked the horn again, holding it down longer this time. The driver of the Subaru stuck a hand out the window and flipped off Victor. Road rage had always been a struggle for Victor, and it reared its ugly head now. He saw red and inched the SUV forward to tap the Subaru's bumper. Not hard enough to make the other driver lose control, but more than enough to send a warning.

The Subaru slowed down even more. It managed to get back in the right lane, but left no space for Victor to merge, even though a sixteen-wheeler barreled toward them in the oncoming lane. With no other choice, Victor swerved left onto the shoulder to avoid a head-on collision. Once the semi passed, the car behind the Subaru dropped back to let Victor merge back into the proper lane.

"That idiot! I could kill him right now and not lose a moment's sleep," Victor fumed.

The highway widened to two lanes on both sides temporarily for an upcoming exit. Victor took the opportunity to pass and switched lanes. The Subaru saw his move and cut in front of him. Every time Victor switched lanes, the Subaru moved to stay ahead of him. Victor didn't know what kind of game they were playing, but he was beyond tired of it. He didn't care about a ticket; it was the apocalypse after all. The highway became one lane in both directions again. Victor saw slower cars again in the right lane and oncoming traffic, so he shifted onto the right shoulder and hit the gas. Once again, the Subaru blocked him and slowed down, forcing Victor to drop his speed or crash. Victor honked his horn again.

"What is this guy's problem?" Victor shouted, his rage turning his face a blotchy shade of red.

"I don't know, but be careful," Dale said.

"I *am* being careful," Victor growled through clenched teeth. "We just need to get around this jerk."

As the Subaru and Victor sped up to get around the slower moving cars, the Subaru swerved a little, but got the car under control.

"Damn, there's a driveway over a ditch. I gotta get over or we're gonna crash," Victor said as he gripped the steering wheel harder.

The Subaru couldn't speed up to get past the car it drove be side, so the Subaru tried to slow down to move behind it, yet Victor was right there on the Subaru's bumper. With little other choice, the Subaru kept driving trying to slow down. It signaled desperately to merge back into traffic. Victor forced his way back onto the road and was able to speed up and ride beside the Subaru, preventing it from merging.

Victor smiled and gestured at the Subaru driver as the distance shortened between it and the possibility of crashing. The Subaru driver tried to speed up again and force his way back into traffic, but it was too late. The Subaru's right tire went into the ditch and hit the driveway head-on.

Victor smirked. "I believe that's what you'd call poetic justice."

"I think that thing that car hit is called a culvert, Dad," Chuck said.

A Good Samaritan stopped to help the Subaru driver, while still approaching, a female zombie ran from a nearby house. She dove into the shattered passenger window after the Subaru's injured driver. The Good Samaritan ran up to the driver side door and yanked it open. He then tried pulling the female zombie out of the driver side door. With a mighty yank, he pulled on her and the sudden lack of resistance sent them both stumbling into traffic, where a sixteen-wheeler smashed into them both.

Chuck winced. "That was gross."

They drove on, letting the incident slip from their minds as other concerns took precedence.

"We seem to be keeping ahead of the zombie virus so far," Dale said. "Let's try to put some more distance between us and the outbreak."

"That's the thing," Bernie said, speaking up for the first time in a while. "I don't think we're outrunning it. We all saw the news. It's already spread across America and to other parts of the world, too.

We don't know if things will be any better in Texas. We're only hoping it'll be."

Dale turned around and shot a nasty glare at Bernie. "Well, would you look at that?" he said with sarcastic wonder. "He can still talk. And here I was enjoying the silence."

Bernie met Dale's glare with one of his own but said nothing.

Victor continued driving, taking Highway 287 south toward the Texas border. They passed Hwy 412 junction. Suddenly, there was a loud, popping noise and the Equinox jerked hard to the right. Victor overcorrected and the SUV started fishtailing.

Victor cursed and gripped the wheel tightly as he turned into the skid, working to keep the vehicle from rolling. Once the SUV was under control, Victor spotted a large open gravel area on the left side of the road and decided to pull over, the blown tire thudding against the undercarriage with every rotation. He brought the vehicle to a stop and shut the engine off.

"We were so close," Victor gritted his teeth, slamming his fist into the steering wheel several times, hitting the horn once. He sighed.

Dale jumped into action. "Everyone out. We need to get that tire changed and the horn will draw in any zombie in the area. Chuck and Bernie, you two keep watch front and back for any zombies."

"Or any more morons who think they can steal from us," Victor grumbled as he climbed out of the SUV.

The younger men took their positions and drew their guns just in case. Their journey so far taught them they had to be prepared for anything. Dale went to the back of the SUV. He moved things around in the bed so he could get to the compartment that housed the spare tire and the tools he needed to change a tire.

"I'll change the tire, Victor," Dale said, his voice steady and calm. "You go stretch your legs for a minute."

Victor nodded. He needed a minute to get himself together. The constant rage bubbling just below the surface was starting to cause him serious problems.

None of them could afford for him to fall apart now. "Thanks, brother."

Dale got to work with the jack while Victor grabbed himself a drink and something to eat while he paced next to the SUV.

"Zombies," Bernie said flatly.

Chuck turned around to look. There was a sizable group about three hundred yards away but approaching fast from the subdivision not too far from the highway. He counted twenty of them.

"Oh, man!" Chuck said, his voice shaky. "There's a pack of them coming right at us. Get a move on, Dale. We need to go now!"

Victor pulled a shotgun from the trunk and looked over at his friend. "We'll take care of them. You just get that tire changed." He turned to Bernie. "You get our six."

Bernie nodded and stood watch while Chuck and Victor opened fire. They took down three zombies, but the noise only made the others run faster.

"Dale, you have got to move!" Chuck shouted.

"I hear you," Dale said. "I'm going as fast as I can."

Chuck and Victor continued shooting into the incoming horde. Bernie kept his gun drawn as he scanned the areas for zombies coming in any other direction, but as the horde got to sixty yards away, he turned and opened fire, too. Less than half the zombies still ran toward them growling.

"Dale!" Victor called. "How's that tire coming? We need to get out of here."

Dale released the jack and the Equinox dropped. "I got it! Almost done. Get ready."

He pulled the jack out from under the SUV, catching his left arm on something from the undercarriage. He ignored the stinging pain and threw everything into the back of the vehicle. Dale turned back to check on the others and saw six zombies just ten feet away. He drew his gun and started shooting.

With Dale in the fight too, they soon cut down four more zombies, leaving just two. One of them ran for Bernie, but he kicked it in the gut and they both stumbled away from each other. With little distance between them, Bernie shot the zombie in the head.

The other zombie ran for Victor. It lunged for him, and Victor quickly held both ends of the shotgun to act as a barrier. He then shoved the sideways barrel into the zombie's mouth. While he wrestled with the ravening beast, Bernie took the opportunity to calmly stroll up and shoot the zombie point-blank.

Victor sucked in deep breaths, trying to calm his racing heart as he realized how close to disaster he'd been. He looked at Bernie with gratitude in his eyes, but Bernie was back to his thousand-yard stare. Victor clapped him on the back.

"You saved my life, Bernie," Victor said.

Bernie mumbled something and turned back toward the SUV. Chuck saw more zombies approaching in the distance, drawn by the sounds of the gunfire. He popped Bernie on the arm with the back of his hand to get his attention.

"Let's get out of here, guys," Chuck said urgently.

They all hopped into the SUV. Victor passed his shotgun to Chuck, who then secured the shotgun in the trunk as the others got settled.

Victor hurried and pulled back onto the highway. Chuck passed a box of 9mm bullets to Dale while Bernie grabbed a box of ammo for himself. The three reloaded their weapons and backup magazines. Chuck then got Victor's handgun and backup mags and reloaded his too.

Part Four: Zombies

Chapter Ten

Oklahoma-Texas Border

Saturday, May 12, 19:35

Dale napped while Victor continued driving. Bernie couldn't sleep, so he watched the scenery and carnage silently through the windows. Chaos and death ruled everywhere he looked. Victor weaved through wrecks, zombies, and the occasional survivor begging for help. He stopped for none of them. Chuck tried to engage Bernie in conversation a couple of times but got no response. Bernie retreated fully into his own mind. Chuck eventually gave up and tried to sleep.

"We're getting close to the border," Victor said. "I don't know what we'll find, but we need to be prepared for anything."

Chuck woke up as Dale nodded. "It's Texas. There are more gun owners there than anywhere else in the country.

They will have safe places where people were prepared. It's all gonna be worth it when we get to Texas."

Indeed, as they approached the Texas border near Kerrick, they could see a thick wooden gate across the road. Fifty yards behind the gate, they saw crews working on a tall wall that stretched off to the west as far as they could see. Solid-looking welded steel slat frames that extended fifteen-foot vertically in the air with barbed wire strung along the top and bottom. Between the gate and the wall, they saw dozens of men and women armed with shotguns and handguns on either side of the road, many standing guard atop their pickup trucks.

Victor slowed the SUV down as he got closer. "Looks like you were right, Dale. Everyone, hands off your guns, and show them your hands. I don't want to get shot before we even make it across the state line."

The others made sure their handguns were covered by their shirts and rolled down their windows to put their hands out as Victor brought the Equinox to a complete stop.

Six men stepped from behind the gate and stood with weapons pointed at the SUV while a tall man in jeans, black t-shirt, and a cowboy hat approached the driver's side window.

"Well, hello strangers," the man said. "My name's Sean. What are your names, and what brings you fellas to Texas?" He held up a clipboard and pulled out a pen.

"I'm Victor, and this is my good friend, Dale, my son, Chuck, and his friend, Bernie," Victor said, pointing to each person in turn. We came from Aurora, Colorado. Things are bad there. We thought Texas might be a safe place."

Sean eyed them skeptically. "What makes you think Texas is any safer than Colorado?"

"Well, besides Texas having its own water supply and an array of crops growing here, there's a strong infrastructure here that also produces bullets and guns," Dale said. Then, while pointing past the gate, Dale said, "I also can see your people putting up a damn fine-looking wall to keep out the zombies."

"Mhmm," Sean nodded. "Zombies and unwelcome people, but you're not wrong. Why should we let y'all into Texas?"

"We're hard workers and we can pull our own weight," Victor answered. "We have guns, too, and we're all pretty darn good shots. We already know to aim for the head to put the zombies down, too."

Sean gave him a sarcastic smile. "Everyone knows that. But we can use hard workers, and there are never enough guns." He nodded. "I'll let you in, although before I do, I'm going to need everyone to step out of the vehicle."

Victor furrowed his eyebrows. "What for?"

"We just need to make sure no one was bitten or scratched," Sean said.

"Well, I can guarantee you we're all fine," Victor said with a confident smile and nod.

"Oh, that's nice," Sean said. "I'd love to just take your word for it, but the people on the other side of that wall depend on me to make sure. How about y'all just hop on out and let me check for myself?"

138

He dropped his hand to the pistol at his belt. "You're more than welcome to turn around and go back the way you came."

Victor shook his head. "Come on, guys. Let's get this over with."

They all climbed out of the SUV and spread apart while Sean's men trained their sights on them.

"Michael, you check those two over there," Sean said, pointing at Dale and Chuck. "Greg, you get these two."

Sean's men did as they were told, making the newcomers strip down to prove their bodies were clear of any injuries that might mean they were infected.

"He's been scratched!" Michael shouted as he jumped back, pulled out his gun, and pointed it at Dale's head.

"Not by a zombie!" Dale said. "It's from the undercarriage when I changed the tire!"

"Shut up," Michael said, kicking Dale in the back of the knee to make him fall to the ground.

"What about the other guy, Michael?" Sean asked.

"The younger one is clear," he answered.

"Keep your gun on them," Sean said. "How about you, Greg? Any scratches or bites on these two?"

"No, they're clear," Greg said.

Sean turned back to Victor, a disappointed look on his face, "Victor... the trust between us had been broken". He didn't bother trying to hide the sarcasm in his tone. "I want you to know that your lies hurt my feelings." He put a hand to his heart and shook his head. "Michael, bring those two over here."

They herded Dale and Chuck over at gunpoint and the four men formed a line alongside the SUV as they put on and adjusted their clothes. Bernie was closest to the vehicle with Chuck on the other end.

"I'll tell you what, Victor," Sean said, pacing slowly in front of them. "I'm feeling generous today. I'll let you and the other two into Texas, but you've got to put your buddy down before he turns."

Victor shook his head in denial. "What? No!" Victor said, shocked. "He wasn't scratched by a zombie. It's just a minor scratch from the SUV.

We got a flat tire near Boise City. Dale changed it while we took care of the zombies. None of them even got close to him."

"That's an outstanding story and I'd sure love to believe it," Sean said. "But I just can't take that chance. People are turning at all kinds of different rates. Shoot him in the head and come into Texas, or you can all leave together."

"Please, no," Victor pleaded. "He's like a brother to me."

Sean shrugged. "You're not the only one with brothers. I'm still waiting, but I'm losing patience."

"Sean, please listen to me," Victor said, his voice taking on a desperate tone. "Dale. Wasn't. Bitten."

"I'm standing right here, fully human and in my right mind, telling you I wasn't bitten," Dale said. "I changed that tire like thirty minutes ago. I would have turned by now."

"In that case, y'all can just load up into your vehicle and be on your way," Sean said. "But the only way you're getting into Texas is if you shoot him."

Victor shook his head. "Please listen. It wasn't a zombie scratch. He got it from— "

"From changing a flat tire," Sean interrupted. "Yes, I can hear."

"Can't we quarantine him or something to prove it's not a zombie scratch?" Victor asked.

"I'm not willing to put my people in danger for a possibility," Sean said, shaking his head. "We have to think about ourselves first so we can help others later."

"Please," Victor begged. "Why are you doing this?"

Sean yawned. "I'm getting bored. I don't have time for compassion. This is a new world, gentlemen. Last chance. Shoot him and join us on the other side of the wall or be on your way and take your chances."

"I'll shoot him," Bernie said, speaking up at last. He stepped forward as he went for his gun but stopped when Michael caught him in his sights.

"Hold it right there," Sean commanded, holding out his hand in a stop motion.

"Thank you for volunteering, but I want Victor to do the honors."

"And if I shoot *you* instead?" Dale growled.

"Well, that would be a shame, to put it simply," Sean said. "See, if you shoot me, my buddies here wouldn't be too pleased about that. They just might shoot you all in the legs, tie you to my truck, set you on fire, and drag you until the fire goes out. They wouldn't kill you, of course. But they would cut you loose a good way from the Texas border, helpless and hobbled. But I don't know. I'm just spitballin' here.

"What is wrong with you?" Victor asked, shaking his head in disbelief.

Sean shrugged and rolled his eyes. "I don't have to explain myself to you. It's my job to ensure my section of the wall is built and that the virus doesn't get into Texas through my area. That's too important to risk for one man."

Dale moved his hand to the gun at his waist. Sean saw the movement and gestured for the others to point their guns at Dale.

"You're going to die regardless," Sean said. "Do you really want your friends to die with you?"

"He would have already turned if it was a zombie scratch," Victor repeated, trying desperately to reason with Sean.

Dale pulled his gun, but before he could raise it fully, a shot rang out. Dale dropped to the sunbaked pavement with his gun falling beside him. Victor looked around in shock, searching for the shooter. His eyes settled on Bernie, who had his gun drawn and his finger still on the trigger.

"Noooo!" Victor screamed.

"I'm not willing to die for him," Bernie said flatly, his voice lacking all emotion.

"What have you done, Bernie?" Chuck shouted. "How could you?"

"Like I said," Bernie continued in the same tone. "I'm not dying for him." He holstered his gun and turned toward Sean. "I just saved your life. Will you let us in now?"

Sean looked surprised. "I reckon you did. I'll let you three in. You can rest up the rest of today.

144

Tomorrow, we'll put you to work. Once our section of the wall is built, we'll set you up with a place to live inside Texas. Until then, you'll be guests of the Home Town Inn down on 54. Victor, follow me in your vehicle. Michael, take your truck and follow behind them. Let's escort our new friends to their temporary home."

Chuck walked toward the passenger seat, but Victor stood his ground glaring at Bernie. He grabbed the younger man and slammed him against the Equinox. "I oughta shoot you right now."

Chuck turned around and jumped between them. But Bernie didn't shy away like he normally would have. "You could," Bernie said, his demeanor calm. "But just remember we are in this situation because of you. All of this was your idea. Your message." Bernie threw up his hands to gesture all around them. "You started all of this, Victor. You are the reason for the zombies."

Sean looked puzzled at the comment but shrugged it off. People tended to get a little crazy during stressful situations and say some wild things. Victor seemed to lose the wind in his sails, calming down fast.

"How could you say something like that?" Victor said in a harsh whisper. "Each of us had a hand in this mess. We did this. *WE,* do you hear me?" He raised his eyebrows to emphasize his point.

"Are you guys gonna kiss and make up over there, or what?" Sean asked. "Because you're about to spend at least the next month in the same small hotel room. Load up in the vehicle and we'll escort you over. Let's go. Daylight's wasting."

Bernie turned away from Victor and opened the back door, but Victor slammed it closed with a thud. "He's not getting in my vehicle," Victor called to Sean.

"I don't care about your dang feelings," Sean said, getting frustrated. "I said to load up in that car. I truly don't like to repeat myself, Victor, and you're making me do it far too often." He looked over to Michael and said, "It's like talking to toddlers for crying out loud."

"I might not be able to do it right now..." Victor warned.

He turned away and got into the driver's seat, staring dead ahead and not acknowledging Bernie at all when he climbed into the back passenger seat while Chuck got into the front passenger seat. Then Victor turned around to stare at Bernie with a murderous glare.

"But I will kill you for this, Bernie." Victor nodded once and turned back around to drive.

Chuck closed his eyes and let out a long, slow sigh as he felt helpless to resolve the tension between them. He knew his dad well enough to know how stubborn to a fault he was. Bernie should not have shot Dale, but there was no other way. Dale had to die. On the other hand, Chuck wasn't sure about this new Bernie he was dealing with. They saw a pickup truck park next to Dale's body. Two men hopped out and loaded the corpse into the back.

Victor felt the sharp agony of loss as he watched them load Dale's body. He blinked away the tears stinging his eyes and followed Sean's truck through the wooden gate then passed the steel wall with Michael right behind him. Their small caravan traveled down the highway for a couple of miles before turning left onto highway 54.

Eventually, they saw a sign welcoming them back into Oklahoma.

"Why are we leaving Texas?" Chuck asked, sitting up to pay more attention to their surroundings.

"I don't know. This Sean guy is a bit off," Victor said. "Stay sharp and keep your eyes open. Let's see what he's playin' at. It sure would be a shame if Bernie killed Dale for no reason."

Bernie, who'd been staring out the window, turned to look at Victor. "*We,*" Bernie said with emphasis, raising his eyebrows.

Victor twisted his neck to look back at Bernie as he gritted his teeth, his face turning red, then turned back to look at the road. He reached for the gun at his hip. Chuck saw his movement and grabbed his wrist to hold it down.

"Dad, stop!" Chuck cried. "Don't kill Bernie. And Bernie, stop antagonizing him! Will you two just stop it already?"

They were silent for the rest of their ride. After ten more minutes, Sean pulled into the parking lot for the Home Town Inn. A pickup truck sat parked on either side of the main entrance.

Several other trucks sat in the parking lot with people standing guard in the beds. Each held a rifle and wore a handgun on their hip. Sean parked and got out of his truck. He signaled for the three men to stay put in the SUV as he went inside the hotel.

Sean exited the lobby a few minutes later and stopped to speak to a man next to the entrance, then sauntered over to Victor's SUV and met Michael at the driver's side window.

"Okay, fellas," Sean said, looking at all three men. "You'll be staying here as you help build this section of the wall. We're actually in Oklahoma right now, but that's only a formality. There's a few things we wanted to claim for Texas, and I don't expect the Oklahoma governor to have much to say about it," He laughed.

"I don't think he has much to say at all these days," Michael said, grinning.

"If you're feeling hungry, there's a diner up the road by the name of Texhoma Livestock Auction Restaurant," Sean said. "We claimed it for Texas because we can." His grin showed how proud he was of the accomplishment.

He passed over a paper sleeved envelope to Victor.

"Here's your room key. The number is on the paper sleeve. It'll be dark soon, so I reckon I'll leave you fellas to get settled and get some rest. We start work early in the morning."

"After we help build this section of the wall, we'll be allowed to stay in Texas?" Victor asked.

Sean nodded. "Yes. You'll have proved yourselves by then. We'll find you an apartment to share and there will be jobs for all of you. We need contributing members of our new Texan society. All you have to do is put in the hard work."

He patted the truck door and turned to leave. "Y'all have a good night now. Oh, and before I go, I informed the lookout team to shoot you if you try to sneak away." He smiled at them, looking friendly despite his ominous words.

"But you said we could go to the diner down the street," Chuck said, confused.

"Yep. That's a fine dilemma," Sean agreed. "Best of luck to ya. Bye for now."

Sean turned on his heels and walked back to his truck, got in, and left as Michael did the same. Victor, Chuck, and Bernie all yawned and stretched.

They were physically drained from all the action and emotionally drained from all the losses. They climbed out of the SUV slowly, grabbed a few things, and went inside the hotel to find their room.

The lobby had been decorated with raw wood and green accents. They followed the signs on the walls to find their room. There was only one queen-sized bed and a recliner in the corner.

"I did all the driving, so I get the bed and the first shower," Victor said as they set their things down and started to unpack.

Victor moved slowly as he grabbed clean clothes and disappeared into the bathroom. Under the running water, he let the day's emotions wash over him. Once he unleashed the tight hold on his emotions, he was sobbing in seconds. He put a hand over his mouth to quiet the sounds, but both Chuck and Bernie heard him.

"Do you think your dad will share the bed with me?" Bernie asked in a flat tone.

Chuck looked at him like he'd grown another head. "Bernie, just stop it already. I can't believe you shot Dale like that.

You *murdered* him right in front of us. You knew good and well that he wasn't scratched by a zombie, and you shot him in cold blood anyway."

Bernie yawned. "Dale was going to shoot Sean. Then Sean's people would have killed all of us. I'm sorry I had to kill Dale, but I was not about to die for him. Getting into Texas was our only plan. You saw what it was like, we wouldn't make it out there on our own. We don't know how to farm and don't have anywhere else to go. Off-kilter or not, we need these people."

Chuck sighed and ran a frustrated hand through his hair. "I know you're right, but *please* stop antagonizing my dad. You shot his best friend and now Dale's body is out there somewhere. Sean probably had his men dump him in a ditch on the other side of the border like trash. Just put yourself in my dad's shoes for a minute. Please, Bernie. Please just stay as far away from him as you can until he calms down. I don't want to lose my best friend, too."

The bleak, hopeless look in Chuck's eyes got Bernie's attention. "Do you think your dad will actually try to kill me?"

Chuck shrugged. "I honestly don't know. He loved Dale like a brother, but you're right, getting into Texas was our *only* plan. Give him time to see it was your only choice. Dad might be a little emotional right now, but he's always a logical person."

"That's debatable," Bernie quipped sarcastically.

"You see that right there?" Chuck snapped. "Stop being so dang sarcastic all the time. Leave my father alone or he *will* kill you. I don't want to watch you die, buddy, and I don't want to be caught in the middle between you and my dad, either."

"Okay," Bernie agreed. "I'll give him space, and I won't be so sarcastic...for now. You know me, sometimes I just can't help it. It just slips on out."

Chuck narrowed his eyes. "Excuses."

They stopped talking when they heard the water shut off. When Victor exited the bathroom, Chuck took his turn in the shower. Bernie waited out in the lobby, not trusting himself to stay quiet alone with Victor for the moment.

When Chuck called him back in, Bernie took a quick shower and came out to find Chuck and Victor asleep in the bed. Bernie crawled onto the recliner and was asleep in minutes.

Chapter Eleven

Texas/Oklahoma Border

Sunday, May 13, 06:00

The sun was going to rise on an entirely different America than the one they'd known. As dawn broke, Chuck and Victor were awoken by a pounding at the door.

"It's time to get up, newbies! We leave in an hour."

Bernie didn't move and stayed covered up on the recliner. Victor hopped out of bed and started getting ready for the day.

"Ugh, I did not get enough sleep last night," Chuck grumbled. He looked over and saw Bernie still sleeping. He kicked the base of the recliner. "Bernie. It's time to get up."

"I'm awake," Bernie mumbled from under the blanket. "I just don't want to get up."

"We need to get ready, you two. We can't afford any slip-ups today," Victor warned in a low tone, his manner strict and straightforward.

Chuck and Bernie both started moving. Bernie ventured out and managed to secure them some dry cereal, a couple of bananas, and three water bottles for breakfast. They gathered some of their MRE rations and got themselves ready when another hard knock sounded at the door.

"Time to load up!"

Victor, Chuck, and Bernie gathered their things and got into the Equinox. Following the caravan of vehicles, they traveled a few miles until they came to an area where the tall wall ended. Everyone parked and got out of their vehicles, waiting for the day's assignments. Sean strolled to the front of the group and hopped into the bed of a pickup truck so everyone could see him.

"Okay," he said, his voice loud and clear. "We'd like to see the wall get just as far today, if not farther than we did yesterday. Everyone work hard, keep an eye out for zombies in all directions, and drink plenty of water. Those native to Texas know that that sun is nothing to play around with."

Sean pointed at Chuck. "You. You're going to be part of Group Six.

They lift the metal slats into the holes. You'll report to Matt in that monster of a neon green pickup over there." Then Sean pointed at Victor. "You're going to Group Seven. They pour the concrete in the holes to make sure our foundations are solid. You'll be working under Sandra, in the maroon Escalade over there." Sean then pointed to Bernie. "You're joining the water crew. You'll mix Gatorade at the start of the day and drive around with the coolers to distribute drinks to the different teams. Fill up and repeat as necessary. Then clean it all up at the end of the workday."

Sean looked around at the crowd. "Jason, raise your hand." When he saw the raised hand, he pointed Bernie in that direction. "Jason runs the water cart. He'll give you the details on your duties."

With the newcomers sorted, Sean turned back to the crowd. "Alright everyone, work safe, work hard. Keep an eye out and drink plenty of water. Let's get to work and build that wall!" He clapped his hands twice to dismiss them and everyone started splitting into their groups to get working.

Bernie made his way over to Jason and introduced himself.

Jason was an older man in denim pants, a short sleeve dress shirt, and a straw hat. He seemed friendly and grateful for the help. Jason covered all the expected duties in detail and motioned for Bernie to follow him. They went to a utility trailer that was hooked to a John-Deere four-wheeler. Inside a small bed on the back were four massive five-gallon water coolers. Jason handed Bernie orange, fruit punch, and lemon-lime Gatorade flavor packets.

"One flavor for each water cooler. The fourth one is just water," Jason explained. I usually get ice from the hotel before coming over, and there is a restaurant down the street from there that has an ice machine, too. I've already done that today, but I expect you to bring ice with you tomorrow."

Bernie nodded with understanding. "So, will I be driving one of these carts?"

Jason shook his head. We only have the one right now. We're on the lookout for another. You'll be riding with me. When we stop at a team, you work on having cups filled so they can get a drink and get back to work faster. We need to maximize the daylight hours."

They spent a few minutes getting the drinks mixed. Then Jason drove them to the first worksite. When they stopped, Bernie hopped out and got to work right away. He already had a dozen cups filled and waiting by the time workers started to meander over toward him as the workers continued their conversation.

"Well, I think the zombie apocalypse started from a space probe returning to earth," said one of the workers who then reached out to grab a cup of Gatorade.

"No. I bet you it was aliens," said the second worksite member as he emphasized with the cup he grabbed.

"That's absurd. I'm sure it was a crazed scientist at a biotech company who contaminated the water," said the third person at the worksite, then took a sip from their cup.

"Now that's ridiculous," Bernie said quickly. "A guy ate a tainted hamburger and went crazy. This is just a weird mutation of the mad cow disease."

"I got you all beat," Jason smirked. "The zombie apocalypse started because of a woman in the morgue with a monkey's paw,"

The workers just looked at Jason while Bernie laughed through his nose.

As Jason and Bernie finished up and continued their route, Bernie turned to Jason to resume their previous conversation.

"How is it that Texas has a plan in place so quickly?" Bernie asked. "It's only been a few days. How in the world did an area this big get so coordinated so fast?"

Jason laughed. "This is Texas, son. Along with guns, we have more than our fair share of conspiracy nuts, too. Though this one turned out to be true, didn't it? There were people in power who believed there might come a day when Texas needed to defend herself against all outsiders. I don't think they were expecting zombies though, but there were contingency plans in place should the need ever arise. Our governor was one of those people. When the news started reporting strange behavior from patients in different towns, which soon spread to multiple states, he acted immediately and enacted the "Texas Stands" protocol.

Bernie shook his head in confusion. "I don't understand. Why would everyone else band together and act so quickly?"

Jason smiled. "Even Texans didn't understand at first. They thought the governor lost his dang mind. But he ordered the hospitals to release the camera footages of the zombie attacks. There's just something about seeing a person eat another person that makes you sit up and take notice. He ordered all the news stations to play the hospital footage, and police videos, too."

"Can the governor even do that? Order news stations to release graphic footage like that?" Bernie wondered.

Jason shrugged. "I don't rightly know, but he did it. The hospitals were more than happy to release the footage. They just wanted to warn people. I think some of the networks were reluctant at first, but they did it."

Bernie shifted uncomfortably in his seat. The guilt ate at him. He'd been part of bringing about the end of the world.

"The governor had the news show the attacks people filmed on their phones, too. It worked.

Everyone was so terrified, that they didn't even think to question the governor when he revealed a plan to keep them all safe," Jason said. "We had able-bodied people show up in droves to volunteer at every station. The governor shut down air traffic into the state right away, but let planes leave freely. He also ordered all the police and armed forces to systematically look for infected people, and tons of volunteers help with that too. So much has happened in such a short time."

"What about the wall?" Bernie asked. "You've got miles up already. It seems like a lot to accomplish in just a couple of days. Where did you even get all the materials?"

"All of that was a part of the Texas Stands protocol. The whole point was that when the rest of the country or world fell, Texas would still be standing. Every construction project in the state was halted at once and all the materials were seized through eminent domain, not that anyone was fighting it. The plan is to build a wall around Texas, with some extensions elsewhere, as you know." Jason's voice rang with pride for his home state.

"That's going to be a mighty long wall," Bernie said in amazement.

"Yeah, well a wall all the way around was the original idea," Jason said. "Shortly after we got started, the plan changed to the wall around all inhabited areas and an eight-foot-wide, twelve-foot-deep trench in others. Every piece of earth-moving equipment in the state is working round the clock."

"How many groups do you have working on this? Texas has a lot of borders," Bernie said.

Jason nodded. "Yep. Right around three thousand two hundred miles. We've got a hundred teams, each responsible for about thirty-two miles of the perimeter. The ditch crews are working round the clock with guards to protect them so we can secure the empty areas. The zombies can't climb well enough to get out of the ditch once they're caught. We patrol and take them out twice a day, so they don't pile up."

"What about all the people who aren't helping? What are they all doing?" Bernie asked, blown away by how protected Texas seemed compared to everywhere else they'd seen since the zombies first appeared.

"Well, hospitals are still going, now that we've gotten the zombies cleared out of the inside of Texas. But darn near everything else has halted until we have the Texas version of a Maginot Line finished," Jason said. "Farmers are still working, with protection of course. People have to eat."

"I have to say, this section of the wall seems pretty sturdy," Bernie said. "Good enough to keep the zombies *out*."

Jason grinned. "Zombies and people. Texas can hold her own." His pride was clear to see. "We have our own water supply, crops, textiles, bullet *and* gun factories, and our own oil and refineries. We have plenty of horses, too. Around a million across the state. The state of Texas is self-sufficient, and we don't want just anyone coming in to start trouble."

"But more people make the work go faster," Bernie protested.

Jason nodded and slowed the cart to stop at the next worksite. "*Good* people make the work go faster. But it's not like 'no good people' are gonna admit they aren't worth a damn, are they?" He eyed Bernie skeptically.

"In my opinion, we might as well seal ourselves off completely. There's plenty of people out of a job and free to help now. We don't need flight attendants or car dealerships right now. We need builders and soldiers and people to work the body cleanup detail. We need cooks and childcare and sanitation. Texas can support herself. We don't need new people. But y'all sure do need us."

Bernie tried not to be too offended. After all, they committed an act of domestic terrorism when they unknowingly unleashed the zombie virus. He had no moral high ground. "So, Texans just don't care about anyone else? You're just going to let the rest of America get eaten?"

Jason laughed as he shut off the four-wheeler and hopped out to start filling cups. "Well, you're here, aren't you? You said y'all came from Colorado. I know you must have seen how bad it is. We can't save everyone. It's a sad fact, but it's a fact, nonetheless. If we just let everybody in, first off, we're gonna miss something eventually and invite the zombies to the self-contained buffet. We can't have that."

Bernie nodded. "That makes sense enough. And yes, we did get into Texas, but it wasn't without its cost. I had to kill Dale and he wasn't even scratched by a zombie. Sean wouldn't listen."

Jason shook his head, lining up filled cups on the trailer's tailgate. "How would you justify a stranger's life over the hundreds of thousands he swore to protect. It's a harsh policy, but a necessary one. Beyond worrying about zombies, we must be selective because you can get people who only want to cause trouble, those who refuse to contribute, or those who won't recognize the authority in place. Texas is bountiful, but there won't be enough natural resources to last forever, either. That's why we have newcomers like you work on the defensive lines as a trial. You have to earn your place here. Anyone who wants to cause problems is free to do so on the other side of the wall."

"I guess I understand that," Bernie said, passing out drinks as the first workers reached their cart. "I just wish none of this ever happened. I wish it was just a normal Friday night and I was sitting around the table playing cards with my friends, drinking beer, and eating pizza."

He got lost in his thoughts for a second until Jason threw an empty cup at his forehead.

"While our way of life has changed significantly, there will be more normal Friday nights. Well, whatever the new normal turns out to be in the end. You'll still have card games with your friends. I mean, besides the one you shot in the head. But you'll make new friends," Jason said.

Bernie gave Jason a strange look, shook his head, and returned to passing out drinks. "So, you heard about that? News travels fast," he said after a few minute of silence.

"Son, everyone who works under Sean heard about it. News travels fast. Gossip travels faster"

"Well, the fact that I shot my friend to get in and that I'm a hard worker should prove I'm willing to go along with the new Texan way of living," Bernie said. "I'd rather work sentry duty than the fields, but I'll do what I'm told. It's just I'm better with a gun than a plow. Who gets the final say on whether we can stay?"

They finished passing out drinks and cleaning up the mess from the current stop. After packing everything up to move on to the next, Jason climbed back behind the wheel.

"Hey, you see that couple there?" Jason said as he tilted his head towards a man and woman walking back to their worksite.

"Yeah?" Bernie said looking past Jason.

"Those two are preppers from North Carolina," Jason said chuckling. "They flew here a few days before the outbreak happened in order to see where John F. Kennedy got shot."

"And?" Bernie asked while shrugging.

"They are preppers from another state, son. They flew out here and then the zombie apocalypse broke out. All of their guns, bullets, and things gathered for emergency purposes are in the basement of their house in a whole 'nother state. Oh, bless their hearts," Jason said trying to hold in his laugh while casually looking over his shoulder at the couple he pitied. "They said something about being good with a gun.

That's why they got sent to work the border. I haven't found out yet why they didn't fly back when they had the chance."

"Interesting," Bernie said with a grin. "I think I'm starting to figure out how gossip spreads so quickly around here."

"Sean has the final say on if you can stay or not," Jason continued their earlier conversation, ignoring Bernie's last comment. "He reports back to the governor. The captain of each section keeps records of everyone in their group—native Texans originally assigned, newcomers from the outside, transfers between groups, and any deaths," Jason said, clearly proud of his captain's work. "I'm not sure how the other groups are doing, but we're right on track. You know, since you killed your friend to save Sean's life, you'll automatically be granted Texas citizenship. Just don't have any major screwups and you'll be fine." He reached over and patted Bernie reassuringly on the shoulder.

"What about the two guys who crossed the border with me?" Bernie asked.

"They'll have to earn a spot for themselves," Jason replied. "They're helping to build the wall, so that will definitely count as a positive. Just as long as they don't cause any trouble, they should be allowed to stay, too."

Bernie felt comfortable with Jason and let his guard down a bit. His shoulders dropped and some of his fear and anxiety showed. "I think Victor, the older guy I came in with, is going to try to kill me."

Jason grunted. "Son, you shot his friend in the head right in front of him. Do you really blame him? If that were me, I would kill you the first opportunity I got."

"Thanks," Bernie said sarcastically. "That's so comforting. What was I supposed to do, let him kill Sean and then you all kill all three of us? How in the hell does that make any sense?"

Jason didn't miss a beat. "You're welcome, friend. I tell it like it is. There's no reason to beat around the bush. What would killing you accomplish, though? If it eases your mind at all, Victor will get kicked out and have to fend for himself if and/or when he kills you."

Bernie shook his head. "Unsurprisingly, that is no comfort at all." He squinted at Jason, trying to decide if the older man was messing with him. "I can practically see his rage bubbling under the surface. It will only take one thing and we'll get into it. I might have to kill my best friend's dad."

Jason shrugged. "Just do your best to avoid him until he comes to his senses and calms down. If you hadn't shot his friend, he would be dead, his son right alongside him. He will realize that eventually."

They pulled into the next worksite and Bernie caught sight of Chuck working on the wall. His team of three lifted one of the long metal slats into place and made sure it sat level. Further down the line, he saw Victor's team pouring quick set concrete into the holes at the base of the slate. Bernie started filling cups, looking over often at the narrow shoulders of his friend and the surly face of Victor.

They filled cups and passed out drinks. Chuck only had a moment to check-in, but he said the work was going fine. It was hard, but he wasn't afraid of hard work.

Victor, however, only glared daggers at Bernie when he came to get his drink. Bernie held eye contact with him, for a few seconds before he remembered his promise not to antagonize Victor. When he turned back, Victor was gone. They continued on their route, passing out drinks until the coolers ran dry. They resupplied and mixed a fresh batch before heading on to the next work site.

"So, when do you think the wall will be finished?" Bernie asked.

"Well, if everyone keeps to the schedule, and the supply chain holds, we should be finished with everything in about three weeks," Jason said. "We're managing about a mile and a half each day at twelve hours a day, seven days a week. Like I said, each group does thirty-two miles of wall. It's a lot of work, but we can do it. Especially if we keep getting good people from the surrounding states since we aren't getting anyone from inside Texas sent to our group."

"Won't you run out of room at the Inn eventually? Is there a such thing as too many workers" Bernie asked.

Jason shook his head and slowed down at another worksite.

"Nah. Sean keeps some of the newcomers to work here and sends others off to help other parts of the state. The more people we have, the more shifts we can work. And we'll need lots of guards when it's done, not to mention the ditch digging."

As they were filling cups, Jason spotted a man on horseback riding hell-bent toward the worksite, sending a plume of dust into the air behind him.

"Well, would you look at that?" Jason said, pointed to the open terrain and a small figure heading their way. "I think that's one of our scouts. Sean thought it would be smart to have a few scouts out roaming to look out for trouble. It never hurts to have a heads up."

Bernie watched the rider. "It sure looks like he's riding awful fast. Something must be wrong."

Jason agreed. "Something's up. I'm calling Sean on the walkie."

Jason pulled out his radio. "Jason to Sean, do you copy?"

"Go for Sean."

"I'm out at worksite four and one of the scouts is riding up like the devil's nipping at his heels. Something is wrong," Jason said.

Bernie caught sight of something through the dust cloud behind the rider and squinted for a better look. "Jason, we have a problem."

"Sean," Jason said into the radio, unable to hide the fear in his voice. "We've got about thirty zombies following the scout and they are headed right for us. We need backup now! They're about half a mile away."

"Get the workers' attention," Sean said. "Fend them off as best you can. I'm on the way with backup!"

"Everyone! Pay attention!" Jason screamed, but only one worker was close enough to hear him.

Bernie knew there was no time to mess around so he pulled out his gun, then fired one shot into the air. Every head turned toward him. He pointed at the incoming horde. Everyone looked in the direction that Bernie pointed, pulled out their guns once they realized what was going on, and ran to take a fighting position.

The scout saw the weapons aimed toward him, and had the horse make a hard turn to the left.

The workers opened fire at the horde. It was hard to hit them accurately in the head at that distance, but the further away they were the better. Sean arrived about five minutes into the battle and took a quick assessment of the situation. He spread the workers a little further apart to form more of a defensive line, adding his reinforcements to the small army. The horde drew ever closer, though the distance grew smaller with each shot. Only two zombies managed to make it far enough to reach any of the humans. They each lunged and grabbed a different worker.

Prepared for a fight but not entirely skilled at hand-to-hand combat, the workers managed to catch the zombies in an arm lock, avoiding scratches and bites. Sean ran over to the closest grappling pair. Moving behind the zombie, he grabbed a fistful of its hair and yanked backwards, his stomach rolling at the squishy sound the zombie made as the scalp started to detach. Sean wasted no time and pulled out his hunting knife to stab the zombie through the back of the skull.

The monster stopped moving and slumped to the ground. Sean wiped the tainted blood on the zombie's dirty clothes and turned toward the other zombie.

The second worker stumbled and fell to the ground, with the zombie toppling over on top of him. The two continued to wrestle. Before Sean could get close enough to help, another worker ran up and skewered the zombie with a knife to the head. It fell limp onto the worker, who then pushed it off and jumped to his feet.

"Man, that was a close one," the worker said as he wiped zombie blood from his cheek. "Too close."

Everyone around him stood staring in shock as if it hurt to look at him.

"What?" he asked, confused.

Sean pointed to the man's shoulder.

He looked down and saw a bite. He hadn't even felt it in the chaos of the fight. "Aw, hell. This is not how I saw my day ending."

"I'm so sorry, buddy," Sean said. He drew his pistol and shot the man through the forehead with no hesitation.

The scout, having seen the battle was over, returned on his horse and dismounted.

Sean looked at him with disappointment and shook his head. "What in the world were you thinking?" Sean demanded.

"What do you mean?" he asked with a shrug.

"What do I mean? I arrived late, but it doesn't take a genius to figure out what happened here," Sean said in disbelief. "I mean why would you bring that horde of zombies *here*?"

"I don't understand, I nee—" the scout started.

"No," Sean screamed. "You shut up and listen to me. I can explain it to you, but I can't understand it for you. Why. Did. You. Bring. That. Horde. Here?" Sean asked, poking the scout hard in the chest to punctuate each word.

The scout swallowed past a lump in his throat, realizing the danger he was in for the first time. "W-we were on patrol to see if we could find any survivors nearby and bring them back here like you said to, but all we found was zombies. The other scout—he saw someone he knows. I mean, *knew*. He got too close and got bit. His screams drew the other zombies, and we were surrounded before we could get away."

"I understand. Very tragic," Sean said, unsympathetic. "Why did you come *here*?"

"What else was I supposed to do?" the scout asked, starting to panic. "I needed help."

"You needed help?" Sean screamed. "So, it never occurred to you that you were on a horse and could easily outrun a horde of stupid zombies? That maybe it wasn't the best idea to bring a horde of the undead down on the people working *on foot* to build the wall? You could have simply lured them away and lost them in the plain or across the border. Instead, you lead them inside our perimeter and to our workers. A man died because of you!"

"That guy died because of a zombie," the scout declared. "I needed help, Sean!"

Sean punched the man square in the nose, knocking him down to the ground. "You still don't get it, do you? You still don't understand what you did." He exhaled slowly and stared at the ground as he ran a hand through his hair, thinking.

"Go to Wade's group," he said flatly. "Help on body clean-up duty."

"No, please," the scout begged in a muffled, nasal tone as he clutched his broken nose. "I don't want to do body clean-up. I love being a scout."

"You have no survival skills," Sean growled. "You're not smart enough to be a scout. I can't afford to lose men due to incompetence."

"Sean, please," the scout pleaded.

Sean sighed heavily. "Look, you're a hard enough worker. That's the only reason you're being reassigned instead of being thrown out of Texas with no horse and no weapons. I hate to burden Wade with you, but I can't have you in my group. Not after this." He turned toward the others. "Greg, Michael, escort him to Wade and make sure he knows why we got rid of him. Take Michael's truck. Leave the horse."

"But I own that horse!" the scout protested.

Sean whirled around to face him again, fury in his eyes. "Leave the horse! A man lost his life. You're losing a horse. I think you got the better deal."

Michael grabbed the scout's arm and pulled him toward the truck. When they were out of sight, Sean turned his attention back to the workers standing around in shock. He gestured at the gore-strewn ground.

"This is exactly why we need these walls and ditches in place yesterday, people. We need this barrier to protect ourselves, and it's going to take everyone working together to make it happen." He clapped his hands together twice. "Alright, everyone. Let's get this thing built."

Everyone went back to their work.

"Guns! We need all the guns!" Jason screamed, pointing over Sean's shoulder to the direction the scout had come from earlier.

Chapter Twelve

Texas/Oklahoma border

Sunday, May 13, 16:07

Sean saw the massive horde moving toward them and felt like he was going to be sick. There had to be at least a hundred zombies barreling toward them. The horse, sensing the impending danger, reared up and cried out in fear before parting the crowded workers to run in the opposite direction. Sean frantically grabbed the radio from his belt.

"Horde incoming!" Sean called. "I need every available gun on my location now. Worksite four! Get here yesterday or we'll be overrun."

Michael and Greg were still close enough to be within radio range, so they whipped the truck around and went back with the scout. Everyone in the vicinity reported for battle, aside from one person left to defend the hotel and one at the restaurant. If the zombies made it that far, they'd already lost. The group to the east sent men to help.

Everyone formed a line between the zombies and the land they needed to protect. They all fired at the massive horde, taking down zombie after zombie, but the zombies just kept coming. To those in the battle, it felt like the waves of the undead would never end. The air stank of gunpowder and fear, and the grisly sight before them wouldn't soon be forgotten.

"They're getting too close," Chuck screamed, struggling to be heard over the ringing in his ears.

"Just keep firing!" Victor yelled back. "Stay focused."

"Why are there so many?" Chuck asked.

Victor shook his head. "I don't know. They must be from across the border. There's a lot of small towns. Just keep shooting. Don't let any of them through!"

More reinforcements arrived and started shooting right away, but it still wasn't enough to eliminate the unending tide of zombies. The leading edge of the horde slammed into the fighters mere minutes later. Some of the workers were tackled by zombies and struggled to fight them off without sustaining injuries.

The others close by helped where they could while the rest of the line kept firing on the horde.

While Bernie was focused on the horde in front of him, a zombie tackled his blind side and knocked him to the ground. Victor noticed and stopped shooting to walk over and watch Bernie fight for his life.

"Don't just stand there!" Bernie shouted. "Help me!"

"No, I don't think I will. I'm going to stand here and enjoy this. Then I'm going to enjoy putting a bullet in your head after you're bitten," Victor smiled.

Chuck saw his friend's dire situation and ran over to help. "What the hell, Dad?" he demanded when he saw Victor just watching.

Chuck grabbed the zombie's hair and pulled it back to give Bernie some space but wasn't expecting the scalp to come free in his hands. Free from its confinement, the zombie whirled around and sank its teeth into Chuck's forearm.

Chuck screamed in pain as blood poured from the wound. Victor's eyes widened in shock and terror. It had all happened so fast.

Now, his son was going to die. Bernie jumped into action and pulled the knife from his ankle holster to stab the zombie through the eye. He pushed it off and stood up, looking down at Chuck with sad eyes.

"All you two had to do was get along," Chuck said, shaking his head in disbelief as he cradled his bitten wrist. Chuck doubled over in pain as the zombie virus worked through his body.

Victor knelt to put an arm around Chuck. "It's okay, son. It's going to be fine," he choked out around the tears tightening his throat. He reached for his knife to grant his son the mercy of an easy death, but Chuck had already turned.

Chuck sprang for Victor, taking a chunk from his neck before Victor could even react. Bernie turned his gun on Chuck and shot him in the head before getting Victor right between the eyes. Bernie stood there in shock, staring down at the dead men. His eyes wide with disbelief over the past thirty seconds, he didn't move even as destruction and death continued all around him. When another fighter saw Bernie standing still, he clapped a hand on his shoulder and shook him hard.

"Snap out of it, man! You're going to get eaten!"

Bernie snapped out of his trance and lifted his gun to continue firing at the zombie horde. He went on autopilot. Aim. Shoot. Aim. Shoot. The world shrunk to what he could see at the end of his gun's barrel. He shot until his weapon ran empty—then he continued to dry fire until someone shook him again.

"It's over, dude. They're all dead."

Bernie came back to reality slowly, unable to look away from the ragged hole he'd blown in his best friend's head. With the horde finally dead, those left alive breathed a sigh of relief. Twelve men from Sean's crew had died, including Victor and Chuck. All the reinforcements from the crew to the east had survived.

Sean climbed into the bed of the closest truck. "Everyone, listen up!" he yelled to get the group's attention. "We need to get rid of these bodies before getting back to work. What happened here today is a tragedy, but we need to finish this work if we ever hope to be safe. All the bodies must be burned. They are infected."

The whole group was obviously shaken. Someone drove a pickup truck around to gather the bodies. It took half a dozen loaded trucks to clear away all the bodies. The twelve who were human when the fight started were set aside, and the workers came over to pay their respects and count their blessings that they were still alive. The zombie bodies were taken about a mile away and piled before the workers doused them with gasoline and set them aflame. Those who'd fallen in battle received a pyre of their own. Sean brought over the can of gasoline himself from the four-wheeler.

"Wait," he said. "I don't see the scout's body. Where is he?"

"Right here," Michael said, pushing the man forward. The scout looked at Michael wide-eyed.

Sean grabbed him by the shirt. "Do you see now why you shouldn't have come back here? Do you see what you've done?"

"I'm sorry these men died, but I needed help!" the scout whined.

"You are selfish and a liability," Sean said, shaking his head as he looked over the good men and women who'd died. He then looked the scout in the eye, "I'm going to kill you."

"Hold on now, Sean," the scout said.

Sean took a step toward him.

"Wait," he pleaded. "Let's just talk about this."

Sean pulled out his hunting knife and stabbed the scout in the stomach then drug the blade upward to his sternum. The scout let out a short scream of pain that soon died away to bloody gurgles as the man fell to his knees. Sean pulled the blade from his chest and stabbed it down through the top of his skull. Sean yanked the knife out and kicked the dead man back. He flopped to the ground while Sean bent to wipe his knife on the scout's shirt before he put it away.

"Michael, will you please help me add this good for nothin' body to the pile?"

They heaved the body onto the pile with the others and finished dousing them with gasoline. Sean lit the pyre on fire and went back to the four-wheeler.

"Back to work, everyone," Sean said. "We have one more mile to build today, and we don't go home until it's done. Greg's people, you're free to go back to your group.

Everyone was disturbed by the horde attack and Sean's brutal treatment of the scout, but they started back to work anyway. No one wanted to get on his bad side just then. Those who'd come to help from Greg's group headed back toward their vehicles so they could attend to their own tasks.

"Hey, Thornton, wait up!" Nguyen said. "I'm gonna grab a drink from their water cart before we leave."

Thornton sighed, "Would you please stop calling me by my last name? The government has fallen. For all we know, the entire country has fallen except for Texas. You saw the same news I did. I think we can drop the protocol."

"Okay, *Morgan*," Nguyen said, emphasizing the name. "Please make them wait for me. I need a drink."

Morgan grinned. "See? That wasn't too hard, was it, *Thanh*?"

Thanh rolled his eyes and called to the soldier who'd escaped the base with them. "Hey, Thompson! I mean Patrick. Do you need something to drink before we head back?"

Patrick nodded. "Yeah, thanks."

Thanh walked over to Bernie. "Hey, can I get three Gatorades? Any flavor."

Bernie looked toward Thanh, but there was no awareness in his eyes. He clearly wasn't focused on his surroundings.

"Excuse me," Thanh said, snapping his fingers in front of Bernie's face. "Can I get three Gatorades, please?"

Bernie seemed to snap back into reality and blinked several times. He shook his head as if to clear it. "Just serve yourself." His tone sounded as dead as he felt inside. He turned his back on Thanh, who grabbed the drinks and hurried back to the car. He passed out the drinks and climbed into the front passenger seat. They drove off, back to Greg's area to the east.

Bernie sat in the four-wheeler, still in the depths of shock. He filled cups and passed out drinks with Jason for the rest of the day, moving entirely on autopilot. Just after dusk, they cleaned up their work area and packed everything away.

"Oh, no," Bernie said, burying his face in his hands.

"What's wrong?" Jason asked.

"I don't have a ride. I rode with Victor. He was one of the ones we lost today. The keys were still in his pocket when he was burned," Bernie said in despair.

"Oh, man," Jason said sympathetically. "You've had a rough day. You lost your last two friends and now you don't even have a way to get around."

Bernie turned bleak eyes to look at Jason. "Yep, that pretty much sums it up." He sighed heavily. "Can you please give me a ride back to the hotel?"

"Sure, no problem," Jason said.

They got into Jason's truck and drove away.

When they arrived at the hotel, Bernie patted his pockets and groaned. He went through the lobby to the front desk.

"I don't' have my room key. May I have a copy, please?" Bernie asked.

"Oh, man," Jason said again as he walked by. "Tough break."

Bernie got the key and went to his room. He walked in, shut the door behind him, sat on the bed, and let the wracking sobs free.

"My best friend is dead," he said aloud. "Everyone is dead. We started the apocalypse. I just wish things could go back to the way it was. I just want to be sitting around the table playing poker."

Without taking the time to think, Bernie pulled the gun from his holster and cocked it. He put the barrel to his temple and pulled the trigger.

Chapter Thirteen

Texas/Oklahoma Border

Sunday, May 13, 17:20

As they drove back to Greg's group, Thanh's cellphone chimed.

"Someone you know is still alive?" Morgan asked in amazement. "I've been calling and texting my family and friends back home, but no one has responded."

Thanh pulled the phone from his pocket and closed his eyes to savor the anticipation of who might still be alive. He unlocked his phone and saw the text notification at the top of the screen.

"It's from AJ Peters!" Thanh exclaimed. "Oh, my goodness, he's alive!"

Thanh turned in his seat to face Patrick in the back seat. "AJ is the one who texted to warn us not to return to base."

"How is he still alive?" Patrick asked in shock. "How could anyone who was on the base that night possibly have survived? I barely made it out."

"Did you make it somewhere safe?" Thanh read Patrick's text message out loud.

"Yes. Only because you warned me. We drove to Texas. There's a wall going up here. Are you safe? Are you okay?" he read out loud as he typed then sent the reply message.

"I barely made it off base, but I got out. I'm held up in a house near the base. Will try to gather supplies and head to Texas."

"I'll look for a way to get to you and bring you to Texas, too," Thanh responded.

"We have to go get him," Thanh said out loud.

"No!" Patrick said firmly.

"I mean, we could ask Greg if he's willing to let us have some guns, bullets, and gas," Morgan said. "But I think you can already guess what he'll say. That actually sounds like a lot to ask for."

"I know he's your friend," Patrick said. "But he's as good as dead and you know it. We should stay here where it's safer."

"We know he's alive!" Thanh protested. "He can give us his location. We can come up with a plan."

Patrick shook his head. "You two can go if you want, but I'm staying here. You'll never reach him let alone make it back here."

"We saved your life," Thanh said. "You owe us."

Patrick let out a disbelieving bark of laughter. "Owe you? I think the best way to show my gratitude is to continue to stay alive and not throw my life away for nothing. You didn't see what I saw and heard. You didn't see soldiers eating each other. You didn't hear the way people screamed as they were eaten alive. I will not go willingly back into that for anyone."

Thanh shook his head in frustration. "Look what just happened. We are on the border helping to build a wall. But it's not done. We are exposed here. We just had to drop that to help another group being attacked. People *died* and we helped burn the bodies. *Nowhere* is safe anymore. Nowhere."

"Let's just talk to Greg and see what kind of supplies he will give us," Morgan said. "We can make a plan from there."

"I just..." Patrick trailed off. He paused and closed his eyes.

"Listen, Patrick," Thanh said. "Two days ago, everything was a typical day. Now we are in danger every living moment. Having guns and our wits helps, but we could still die at any minute, regardless of where we are. Please, come with us."

"Okay, I guess," Patrick grumbled. "If the group leader will give us supplies. If I'm gonna die regardless, it might as well be on my terms." He buried his face in his hands and said nothing for the rest of the drive.

They returned to their group. Everyone parked and made their way back to their work groups.

"When should we talk to Greg?" Morgan asked. "Now or after work?"

"After," Patrick suggested. "He's already bound to be on edge, and if he agrees, we can head out in the morning."

"Tomorrow morning might be too late," Thanh replied.

"Look, we still have to drive all the way back to base. Even if every road was clear and we ran into no problems at all, we still wouldn't get there until morning. Besides, it's safer to travel in daylight because we'll be able to see the zombies a lot better," Patrick protested.

"I agree. Let's finish work today, and head out fresh in the morning," Morgan said. "Besides, we only just met our group leader. Maybe if we work really hard today, Greg will be more willing to give us what we need."

They worked hard until everyone stopped for the night. They nervously approached Greg as the other workers started for their rooms. Greg was a tall man with long sandy brown hair in a ponytail and a proper English accent. He looked up from the paperwork on his clipboard.

"May we talk with you for just a minute, sir?" Thanh asked.

"It's just Greg, mate. What's up?"

"I'm going to be straight with you," Thanh said.

"I received a text from my friend, and we would like some supplies so we can go get him. We need gas, guns, and ammo."

Greg laughed for a moment until he realized they weren't joking. "Oh, I thought you were taking the piss. No. I won't part with valuable resources and workforce so you can go attempt to rescue one person. It's far more likely that you'll never return. That's a lot to lose. I'm sorry, mates, but that math just doesn't add up." He went back to his paperwork.

"Greg, please!" Morgan said. "This man saved our lives. We wouldn't even be here if it wasn't for him."

"No," Greg said more firmly, looking each of them in the eyes. "Think, yeah? You're reacting out of emotion, and I will not waste resources. I'm being logical and thinking about the greater good. You lot stay here. If your mate can make it to Texas, he'll be welcomed."

"But how are we supposed to save our friend if you won't help us?" Thanh asked, his voice taking on a note of desperation.

Greg shook his head. "Are you mental?

Unfortunately, you can't save him, mates. Carry him in your memories. Ensuring that Texas continuous to stan will ensure those memories live on. Now leave it and piss off." He looked at each of them one last time then walked away.

"Wow," Patrick said, still reeling. "I saw that conversation going very differently."

"You never wanted to go anyway," Thanh said bitterly.

"Could we steal what we need?" Morgan asked.

Patrick shook his head. "Not a chance. Their resources are too heavily guarded. No distraction is going to get the guards looking the other way long enough to get supplies."

Thanh balled a fist against his temple. "No, no, no," he said. "What are we going to do?"

"We could sneak out and take the route to the group closest to Fort Polk. Maybe if we ask the group leader there, we can get the resources we need to rescue AJ," Morgan suggested.

Patrick shook his head again, "She barely let us into Texas, remember?

We had to convince her to give us gas just to make it to this group, where *she* sent us. I highly doubt the other group leaders along the way will be generous. Face it. No one is going to help us or give us what we need. We can't help AJ."

"But he saved our lives. We gotta do *something*," Thanh said.

"Pray for him. It's all we can do," Patrick said, putting a hand on Thanh's shoulder.

Thanh hung his head as the three of them piled into Morgan's car to return to their hotel. Once at the hotel, they took turns showering and climbed into bed. Thanh laid down on one of the two queen-sized beds and set his phone on the nightstand where he could see it. When it rang ten minutes later, he jumped up to grab it, turning on the speakerphone.

"AJ!" Thanh answered in a panic. "Are you okay?"

They heard a choked sob. "I got trapped in a bathroom with no way out," AJ said. "Either the zombies are going to break down the door to get me or I'm going to starve to death.

Either way, I'll be dead. Don't bother trying to come for me. It's far too dangerous."

Thanh could hear AJ trying to hold his composure together, trying desperately not to sound too scared or hopeless. There was a loud noise in the background. AJ yelped and the line went dead.

"He's going to die," Thanh said, his voice flat. "He saved our lives and now he's going to die alone. There's not a thing we can do about it."

Thanh laid back on the bed and stared at the ceiling as his eyes filled with tears.

Chapter Fourteen

Greg's House

Friday, May 25, 20:00

A couple of weeks later, Greg rushed home after the day's work was done. Most of the wall was completed and the people of Texas felt much safer. Life was starting to get to a new normal. A voluptuous woman with long, curly black hair greeted him when he walked through the door. He closed it behind him and wrapped his arms around her, grateful for another day together. He kissed her and smiled.

"I missed you today, Amy," Greg said, gently stroking her face. "I'm going to jump in the shower really quick." Greg said as he walked up the stairs. When he walked out of their bathroom, he found Amy had set out clothes for him.

"I picked out something nice for you to wear, honey," she said. "Let me just put on my jewelry, and I'll be ready."

"Thanks, love," Greg said as he dressed. "I'll just be a minute."

He finished dressing and made his way downstairs to the dining room, where Amy was setting the table with their finest dinnerware. Fifteen minutes later, a knock sounded at the door. Amy answered it, smiling as she stepped back to welcome a short, dark-haired woman.

"Eliza!" Amy said. "Come on in. It's great to see you."

The other woman stepped forward to hug her friend. She was a fit, brown skinned Black woman, long dark brown hair, and a beaming smile. "Thanks for inviting me! It's been too long since I've had a homecooked meal. They put me up in a hotel, so I'd be closer to the build site and the others on my building team, but all that microwave food is driving me crazy. And don't get me started on only eating vegetables and beef jerky during the day. I gotta make time to go back to my house and get my air fryer, but work has just kept me going from sunup to sundown. By the end of the day, I'm just too tired to make the trip."

Eliza slipped out of her jacket and Greg took it to hang in the hall closet. She pulled him into a hug, too. "Thanks, Greg. It's been too long since I came to visit."

Greg smiled, "You're always welcome, Eliza. You know that. Vivian and Stephen should be here any minute. Go sit and relax on the couch."

The three of them got settled in the living room and were chatting happily when there was another knock at the door.

"That must be them," Amy said, getting up to welcome their guests.

"Amy!" Vivian and Stephen chorus together when she opened the door.

Vivian was a short, thin blonde woman with glasses. Stephen stood a few inches taller and had a blonde buzz cut. He pushed his glasses further up his nose and grinned at Greg.

"Mate! It's been too long!" Stephen said, his Australian accent strong.

"Hey, you two. Come on in, dinner should be ready in just a few minutes," Amy said. She pulled them both in for hugs as they entered.

Amy saw the guests to the living room and went to check on the food.

"It's ready everyone. Please make your way to the dining room. I'll be right in to serve," Amy said.

"Wait, where's your plus one, Eliza?" Greg asked as they ate.

She offered him a sad smile. "Well, I went to the grocery store the other day and saw him there holding hands with another woman."

Vivian groaned in sympathy. "I'm sorry to hear that, honey."

Eliza shrugged. "I'm not too upset about it, but I am hurt. I've been spending all my time on the wall and just never had any leftover time for him. But even before all this started, it seemed like there was always something else more important. I just wish he'd found a different way to handle the situation."

"Yeah, I know exactly what you mean," Greg said. "I'm gone before sunrise and return after sunset. When I do finally come home, I eat and go right to bed so I can get up and do it all over again the next day."

"I have to say, I'm glad for the clean-up duty," Vivian said. "We see a lot of gross stuff, and it's beyond heartbreaking, but we get to be together."

"We only work from around eight in the morning to five in the afternoon," Stephen added. "There's enough people on body detail and fewer deaths now, so we even get a proper two days off."

"We'll have to get in touch with the governor and see about getting more people to help on the border. We don't have much left to finish on the wall, but more people mean we'll get done a lot sooner," Eliza said.

"The group west of mine was attacked by a horde two weeks ago," Greg said. "I sent men to help out."

"Oh, no!" Amy said, covering her mouth with a hand in dismay.

Greg nodded. "It was awful. They lost around a dozen men. I didn't lose any of mine, but they asked for some of my people to join them permanently. I have my own tasks that me and my people must finish. None of us can afford to get behind schedule. And to top it off, I had three people from my group ask for some supplies the same day for some suicide mission to save one person back in *Louisiana*." He rubbed his temples.

"That sounds awful, mate. I don't envy your leadership position on the wall. It's a lot safer in the city.

We still have the occasional zombies, but there are no hordes that far from the border. We found one zombie inside a house today. He was eating his wife," Stephen said. "It was disturbing."

"Yes, it was. Thankfully, it was distracted enough that we didn't have a problem killing it, or the victim," Vivian added.

"Well, I'm glad you two are safe," Eliza said. "But can we talk about something else? Like, literally anything other than zombies?"

Vivien brightened. "Guess what I found today?"

"Diamonds?" Amy asked.

"Essendon memorabilia," Stephen guessed.

"Coffee?" Eliza asked with a wistful tone.

"A Kawasaki Ninja ZX-11?" Greg asked.

Vivian shook her head and got up to grab her purse. "Nothing quite as exciting as all that. I found a whole pallet of healthy meal replacement drinks. They were still wrapped up in plastic.

I used to drink these things all the time. They'll be great for working on the wall."

She brought the bottles back to the table and passed them out to her friends. "Taste varies by flavor, but they give you the nutrition your body needs. This is supposed to be a new flavor."

Eliza shook her head when she was offered a bottle. "No, thanks. After watching that one movie, I could never bring myself to drink any of those 'all-in-one' drinks." She made a strange face. "It's people."

Greg laughed. "I remember that one!"

"Come on," Stephen encouraged. "It's healthy for you. This has all the proteins, vitamins, and minerals you need. No people included."

"Nope. Thanks though," Eliza insisted. "It's a hard pass for me."

"Well, we'll take a couple," Amy said. She held out her hands and Vivian passed her three bottles. "Cheers, mate." Amy set them on the counter and went to grab dessert.

The group of friends talked and laughed with one another for a couple of hours, simply enjoying each other's company. Before it got too late, the guests departed for home, leaving Amy and Greg alone.

She leaned against him and sighed. "It was so nice spending time with our friends again. It felt almost normal. Even though you've only been a group leader for a little over two weeks, this is the closest we've had to a date for a long while. We were so busy even before the apocalypse."

Greg kissed the top of her head. "It was nice seeing them. Too bad it took an apocalypse to make it happen. I'd love to get Vivian and Stephen on my build team though."

Amy laughed. "I'm sure Eliza would, too. But I don't think they have any interest in building. You heard them; they want to stay away from the wall. Besides, I think Eliza would fight you for them."

Greg chuckled. "You're probably right. You know, I'm glad the governor chose Eliza to lead the group east of mine. She's good at what she does.

I don't think Vivian and Stephen are too far away either, but I'm not real familiar with the sections further out."

Greg and Amy went upstairs to their room. Greg groaned as he prepared for bed.

"Oh, goodness," he said. "I wish I could take tomorrow off."

"Can't your second in command manage things for one day?" she asked.

He shook his head. "There's not enough people. And it's my responsibility."

She aimed a wicked grin at him. "How much time do you have until you absolutely *have* to be asleep?"

"For you, my love, I have all the time you need," Greg said, looking her over with a loving gaze. He leaned over and stroked her cheek before pulling her closer for a gentle kiss.

"I get to see you every day, but I still miss you," Amy said.

She snuggled closer and wrapped her arms around his neck. He slid his hands around her waist and kissed her passionately. Soon, there was no space between them.

He ran his fingers through her hair, enjoying the soft sighs of pleasure the simple auction elicited.

"I love you," Amy murmured into his chest.

He stretched an arm to shut off the lamp without letting her go, plunging them into darkness. "I love you, too, beautiful. Come here."

Chapter Fifteen

Texas/Oklahoma Border

Saturday, May 26, 05:30

Greg woke the next morning to the sound of his alarm. He still had one arm wrapped around his wife, who snored softly as she lay on his chest.

"I can't wait 'till this bloody wall is done," Greg said as he shut off the alarm.

He rubbed the sleep from his eyes with his free hand and carefully slid out from under Amy. He showered and was getting dressed as Amy woke up.

"Honey, would you like me to make you some breakfast before you head out?" she asked.

"I don't have time, love. Thank you for offering. I have to get moving."

"Take one of those drinks Vivian gave us last night then," Amy suggested. "At least you'll have something in your belly," she said.

He nodded. "Okay. I'll do that." He crossed the room and kissed her before he left.

"I'll make your favorite meal for dinner tonight," she said.

"I can't wait." He smirked as he walked out the room. Amy was an excellent cook, and he loved her food. He knew how lucky he was to call her his.

He grabbed one of the meal replacement bottles on his way out the door and dropped it into his passenger seat as he drove toward the wall. By the end of the day, he was exhausted and hungry. He wanted nothing more than to enjoy a good meal and relax with his wife for a full night's sleep.

"I made lasagna," Amy called from the kitchen when he got home that evening.

"It smells amazing in here," Greg said with enthusiasm.

"So, did you try the drink for breakfast?" she asked.

He shook his head. "I was going to, but a newbie made it to the wall in my section today and he was half-starved. I figured he needed it more. What about you?"

She nodded. "I did try it. The first couple of sips weren't that great, but I figured out I was supposed to shake it first. I started to like it after I did that. I can't quite place the flavor, though."

They sat down and enjoyed Amy's delicious cooking. After they ate, Greg put on a movie, and they snuggled on the couch together before bed. It was a simple, rather repetitive life, but they felt safe and grateful for the chance to be together.

Greg's House

Friday, June 1, 06:00

A week later, Amy came down with a nasty stomach bug. She was holed up in the bathroom, sounding miserable.

"Are you going to take the day off?" Greg asked as he dressed for the day.

"I think I probably out to," she said as she stumbled back to bed. "I would hate to see others feeling like this. I'm sure I'll be fine if I drink plenty of water to flush this out of my system."

"Okay, babe. I'll see if I can find some soup for you. Either way, I'll take care of dinner. You just rest." Greg brushed the hair out of her face. "Do you need anything else?"

She shook her head. "I'll be fine. Quit fussing. Now get out of here, you don't want to be late." She smiled weakly and waved him away.

Greg returned home that night after dark, carrying a container of warm chicken soup for Amy. He didn't see any lights on when he got home. She must still be sleeping he thought.

"Honey, I'm back," he called as he walked through the door and turned on the lights. He didn't hear a reply. So, he dropped everything off in the kitchen and walked up the stairs to the bedroom. Amy laid on the bed, still sleeping.

"Hey, babe," he said, gently as he turned on the bedroom light. She didn't react right away. "Amy, honey. How do you feel?"

She sat up slowly and turned to face him. Her skin had gone a pale, chalky color. Her lips were blue, and the irises of her eyes were white. Greg shook his head in denial.

"Oh, baby, no. Not you. Please not you," he muttered.

She came from around the bed and lunged for him, teeth bared. He grabbed her wrists as she reached for him and struggled to push her toward the bathroom. He managed to get her inside and slammed the door shut. The zombie, who had been his wife, banged on the door growling in frustration.

Greg slid to the floor as tears flowed down his cheeks. He dropped his head into his hands and sobbed.

"Not you, Amy. Not you."

He turned and slammed his fist against the door. The zombie got riled up and banged harder. Greg stood up, checked the rest of the house for any other zombies, then pulled the phone from his pocket to send a message to warn the others.

Minutes later, Greg pulled himself out of his daze to answer a knock at the front door.

"What's wrong?" Eliza demanded. "You look terrible. I came as soon as I could."

"It—it's Amy," he said, his voice breaking with sorrow. "She's in the master bathroom."

"Is she okay?" Eliza asked hesitantly.

Greg stepped out of the way to let her in. "She's a zombie," he said, then burst into tears.

"What?" Eliza asked as her eyes went wide. "How is that even possible?"

"I don't know," he said through the sobs. "I don't know. She said she had some kind of stomach bug and was going to stay home.

There weren't any zombies in the house or any sign of a struggle. I don't know what happened."

"Do you want me to take care of it?" Eliza asked, placing a comforting hand on his shoulder.

He nodded. "Please. I can't do it, Eliza." His tears flowed freely. "I can't bring myself to do it. Not even to free her from that hell."

"Don't worry about it, my friend," she said. "I'll release her."

She hugged Greg and turned to walk upstairs. Eliza pulled her knife as she got close to the master bedroom. She stepped closer to the bathroom door, where she clearly heard Amy pounding on the door. Eliza stood near the hinges and took a few deep breaths to center herself.

Eliza raised her knife as she moved closer to the doorknob and opened the door slightly. With the door open, the zombie grabbed the edge of the door and tried to force it wide, but Eliza had a solid grip. Amy stuck her head through the gap, ravenously searching for someone to eat. Eliza didn't waste a second.

She used the door to trap Amy's head in place and brought her knife down into the top of her skull. Amy stopped moving and slumped.

Eliza cried silent tears as she pulled her knife free and cleaned it on Amy's shirt. She sheathed her knife and struggled to lay Amy flat on the bathroom floor so she could cover the body.

Greg wandered in when he heard the commotion stop. Eliza turned to look at him, hating the raw agony of loss in his eyes.

"I don't know how this could have happened," he said. "She was never bitten. Never scratched. I'm not sure she even saw a zombie up close."

Eliza shook her head. "I don't know. I'll help you dig a grave out back. She deserves that much."

Working together, they wrapped Amy's body in a bedsheet and carried her to the backyard. They dug a hasty grave as deep as they could manage and gently laid Amy to rest.

"Vivian and Stephen should be here for this," Greg said.

"I've been calling and texting them, but I haven't been able to reach either of them."

"They'll be furious that we didn't tell them about Amy. Let's just go over there and check on them. I think they are supposed to be off today," Greg said.

"Greg, I've got a bad feeling about this," Eliza said.

He nodded. "Me, too."

They got into Eliza's car and drove over to their friends' house. "I'm so sorry, Greg," Eliza said eventually, breaking the oppressive silence. "I don't know what to say."

"I'm not sure there is anything to say," Greg muttered. "I just wish I knew how this happened and make sense of it all."

Eventually, the two arrived at their friends' house.

"Well, the garage door is down," Eliza said. "I guess let's go see if they're home."

After parking, Eliza went to her trunk. She handed Greg a handgun and took a handgun for herself. They took a moment to load their guns then walked up to the front door and rang the doorbell. It only took seconds for Vivian and Stephen to make it to the front of the house. One banged hungrily on the door, while the other pounded on the window.

Eliza gasped. "No! How?"

Greg and Eliza looked at each other. "I don't know, he said. "I'm not sure what Vivian and Stephen have done since we saw them last, but I *know* Amy wasn't bitten."

"What else could it be?" Eliza asked, wracking her brain for ideas. "Food? Water?"

Greg shook his head in denial. "Amy and I eat the same things. We may not always eat together, but we always ate the same food. We ate dinner together and sometimes eat leftovers for lunch. Depending on what we had."

"What about breakfast?" asked Eliza.

"Not breakfast, necessarily. I usually have to run off in the morning and don't eat."

Their friends continued pounding on the door and window for release, snarling savagely at their potential meals.

"We're going to figure this out, Greg, but first, we have to take care of Vivian and Stephan," Eliza said then covered her mouth as if it hurt to say the words. "We can't leave them like this."

Greg nodded. Eliza grabbed Greg's arm. "I have a thought, Greg. Vivian handed out those nutrition drinks last week. Did you drink any of it?"

"No," he said. "I planned to, but I had someone show up to my group half starving, and I gave it to him."

"Okay. So, if you let him into Texas and he wasn't bitten, but is now a zombie, it must be the drink," Eliza reasoned.

Greg couldn't fault her logic. It made more sense than any other idea he had. "I'll call the guards at the hotel and send them to check on the new guy." He pulled out his phone and made the call. "One of my guys is going to check on the newbie. I gave him heads up just in case. We'll know shortly."

"In the meantime..." Eliza said, gesturing to their zombified friends.

Greg got the spare key from under a fake rock and unlocked the front door. "You make sure you're at least thirty feet back. I'll open the door and try to draw them out. While their attention is on me, you take them out. Please be quick about it. I need to get back to the hotel and stop this from becoming an all-out disaster."

Eliza took her position and unholstered her gun, "You draw them out. I take them out."

"Ready?" he asked, drawing his own weapon. She nodded.

Greg threw open the door and took a running leap off the porch. He landed and spun and looked back. Vivian was the first out the door, with Stephen right on her heels. They both stumbled over the side of the porch and fell in a heap. Eliza shot at Stephen but missed. He got to his feet rushed towards her. Her hands shook so badly that her next three shots all missed completely. The next one hit him in the shoulder. He spun but turned to run toward her.

Her eyes went wide with fear, but she breathed out, lined up the shot with Stephen's forehead, and squeezed the trigger. The bullet met its mark and he fell hard.

Eliza turned to fire at Vivian, but she realized that she couldn't get a shot without hitting Greg. Vivian ran close enough to Greg to grab hold of his ponytail, which she yanked hard. Greg slipped and crashed to the ground. He quickly spun around on his back and kicked at Vivian as she dove onto him. He knocked her back, but she regained herself quickly and dove for Greg again. Greg raised his arm, with his elbow bent, and caught Vivian at the neck. He franticly fought to keep Vivian's hands from scratching him.

Eliza took a shot but missed, then ran to get closer and aimed her gun at her friend's head. With Vivian's teeth frantically gnawing to bite Greg's face, she never saw Eliza coming. A shot rang out, and Vivian went limp. Greg dropped Vivian's body to the side, then got up unsteadily to his feet and looked at Eliza in shock.

"How can you possibly be that bad of a shot?" Greg asked. "We all used to go shooting together."

"I'm sorry. It's been a while since I had to shoot a gun, and I'm a little rusty, especially since my section of the boarder doesn't get that many zombies. I didn't think I'd be that bad," Eliza said.

Greg panted, trying to catch his breath after the excitement. "Seriously? That was *way* too close though." Greg started to take slow deep breaths with his hands on his knees when his phone rang. He answered.

"You were right, sir. The new guy was a zombie. We put him down," the voice said overt the phone.

The conversation was brief, and Greg soon hung up looking grim. "Well, that confirms it." Greg then started texting on his phone. "I'm texting some men now to come and bury Vivian and Stephan. We have to get back to the border to help contain this situation."

Eliza and Greg started to hurry towards her car when Eliza stopped, "No. We need to warn the governor so he can warn the whole state."

"All of Texas is in grave danger," Greg said.

Eliza pulled out her cellphone and called Lieutenant Governor Calhan.

She was on the phone for a moment explaining the situation, then hung up.

"Good news is he believed me. He doesn't want to take any chances and is going to have the warning broadcasted everywhere on a loop so no one will drink that meal replacement drink," Eliza said as she put her phone back in her pockets.

"Okay, the way you say that makes me think there's bad news too. What else did he say?" Greg said as his shoulders drooped.

"He said since we 'showed such bravery in the face of danger', he wants to reassign us to assist the research team. We need to recruit a few more workers of our choosing to go with us first thing Monday morning," Eliza said as she shook her head as she rubbed her eyebrow.

"That sounds more like a punishment then a reward. Although I could really use the two days to grieve, I started my section of the wall, and I would really like to finish. We're so close. Plus, we don't know how we'll be helping."

"Calhan's gonna text me the research team info. I'll contact whomever tomorrow morning," said Eliza as she looked at her friends' dead bodies then quickly turned away. "I say we don't take the initiative or try to be clever next time something happens."

"Agreed," Greg said then sighed. "We both have very good workers on our build team. Who should we choose to come with us?" Greg said as he tried to position himself between Eliza and their friends' bodies. "I don't want to do the build team a disservice."

"Come on. I think our teams can handle things without us. I'll drop you off at your place. I'm too exhausted and I just can't."

"I don't think I can sleep at my place. At least not just yet," Greg said softly.

"I understand. How about I just take you back home so you can grab a few things, then you can stay in one of my spare bedrooms? If I'm getting reassigned, I'm going to sleep at my house."

Greg nodded as he shuffled towards the car.

As they were walking, both of their phone's Emergency Alert System sounded. They each checked their phones and acknowledged the warning in order to stop the chime. Once they got into Eliza's car, she received a text and checked her phone.

"Calhan just sent me the contact information for the research team," Eliza said then started driving toward Greg's house after putting her phone away. They chatted and joked about what they'll be doing for the research team. Once at Greg's house, Eliza parked in the driveway.

"I'll just grab a few things and be right back. I'll take my car and follow you," Greg said has he got out of the car.

"Okay," Eliza said then waited in her car listening to music. Ten minutes later, the garage door opened. Greg was sitting in the driver's seat of his car and waved out the window to Eliza. They both got on the road and headed to Eliza's home.

Once at Eliza's house, Eliza and Greg parked in her garage and went inside. Eliza pointed to the spare bedroom for Greg to use, then went to the master bedroom and closed the door.

She took a shower and started getting ready for bed as Greg used the extra bathroom and started doing the same. Once done, they both passed out on the bed in their rooms.

Eliza's House

Saturday, June 2, 08:00

The next morning, Eliza awoke to the smell of breakfast. She got up and ready for the day, then went to the kitchen.

"Thank you for cooking breakfast, Greg. How did you sleep?" Eliza asked. Greg looked up with a hurt smile, looking as if he was fighting back the tears, then went back to cooking.

"I'm sorry," Eliza said. "This whole apocalypse has got us stressed out, and we can't properly grieve or take time off for our wellbeing."

"I'm sure once the wall is finished and the research team gets what they need, things will calm down. We just need to push a little longer."

Greg finished cooking and turned off the stove. He then proceeded to make a plate for both Eliza and him. They sat at the table and started eating.

"What do you think is the probability of us being able to say 'no' if we don't like the assignment the research team gives us?" Eliza asked.

"What do you mean?"

"The sound of Calhan's voice. It seemed like, although he was asking, we were actually being *told* that we had to work for the research team."

"I'm sure we can turn down the offer if we don't like it, we'll just be reassigned to something worse."

"I'll call the contact person for the research team once we're done eating breakfast." They continued talking as they finished eating. Once done, Greg grabbed the dirty dishes and started cleaning up the kitchen.

Eliza pulled out her cell phone and called the contact person. She put the person on speaker so Greg could hear firsthand what the person on the other line had to say. Eliza reached for a pad and pen from the kitchen drawer as the contact person explained in detail what Greg and Eliza needed to do in order to assist the research team. Greg and Eliza shook their heads as Eliza took more notes. All three where on the phone for about an hour as Greg and Eliza interrupted the contact person to ask questions. Eventually, they hung up and sat in silence mulling over the conversation they just had.

"Definitely a punishment and not a reward," Greg said as his shoulders drooped.

"It's a suicide mission."

"Innit. Which group would you like to lead?"

"Always the gentleman. Let me think. I can lead the group going around to get different meal replacement drinks from different states, or travel into Colorado and collect their water at various locations. I don't like either choice."

"Eliza, both are highly dangerous. I think having to go into various warehouses will be more dangerous then collecting water since you can see danger coming in every direction. I want you to go to Colorado and collect their water," said Greg.

"I guess. Well, while I'm in Colorado, I might as well stop at a few warehouses and collect the various meal replacement drinks there."

"Who would even volunteer to come with us?" Greg asked.

"Hey, what about those guys who was willing to drive back to Louisiana to get their friend? Seems like they're willing to take risks."

"Going to get a friend is one thing. Helping the research team is different. People might not be willing to help once they find out what we'll be doing."

"I say we start with putting the word out there and see who'll raise their hand willingly, then pull a Calhan if we don't get any takers," said Eliza then put her hands over her face. Greg reached over and hugged her.

"I'm not even going to lie and say it'll be okay, but we have our wits about us, said Greg.

The End

Epilogue

Governor's mansion

Two Months later

Two epidemiologists sat in an ornate waiting room. Each carried a small briefcase and looked out of place in the bustling's office. The main door to the governor's office opened. Governor Webb saw his guest out and turned to the doctors.

"I'm sorry to keep you two waiting. Please, come in," he said, gesturing for them to join him in his office. The doctors followed him in and took seats across from the desk.

"Doctor Saunders and Doctor Morrow, thank you for coming today. What have your teams learned?"

Doctor Morrow pulled a report from her briefcase and passed it across the desk. "My team could not find a cure for the infected people, so far, sir. But with Dr. Saunders' new findings, we might be able to make some real progress."

The governor turned to Dr. Saunders. "I take it you've discovered what caused all this?"

The doctor nodded. "Yes. We've been working on this almost around the clock. There was some speculation about a chemical theft in Colorado, but it turns out those were just inert Alzheimer's medications. It killed off a bunch of fish, but it didn't cause the zombies. The Texas CDC had a breakthrough and it's made all the difference in the world. We had to do extensive research to confirm, and it meant some risky sample collection, but we now know the exact cause of the zombie outbreak."

"Well, spit it out, man!" the governor said, frustrated.

Dr. Saunders passed over a portfolio from his briefcase. "This shows the chemical compound that was used to cause the undead plague."

Governor Webb thumbed through the portfolio, skimming the pages. He stopped at a photo of a bottle. "Really? I know a couple of people who used to drink that stuff all the time. This stuff has been around for ages. What's different now?"

"The problem was something in the new flavor," Dr. Saunders said. "We haven't nailed down the exact chemical compound yet, but we're working on it."

The governor smiled. "This is good work! It's a shame we will probably never know how or why this happened, but at least we know what did it. I already had crews go around Texas to gather every bottle of this they could find. We'll need a plan on how this product can be safely destroyed."

Dr. Saunders nodded. "With the rest of the world in shambles, I doubt we will ever decipher full answers to our questions. On the bright side, we can say with absolute certainty that the virus has nothing to do with the attempt to taint the Colorado River water."

"Texas is self-sufficient in so many ways, but we need water to survive. We had to know for sure," Dr. Morrow said.

"Well, with this new information we can move forward from here. I already have our top ecologist Dr Clark and top engineer Mr. Caples implementing plan B for water.

Just in case. Hope for the best. Plan for the worst," Governor Webb said.

"Texans have been through so much in such a short period of time," Dr Morrow said.

"Texas would have been overrun from the inside if it wasn't for that tip from the two group leaders in north Texas," Governor Webb said. "Thanks to them, Texas still stands. Three months since the initial outbreak and our defensive line is holding strong. People inside the boarder will be able to continue living their lives in peace inside New America. Now, if you two will excuse me, I have another appointment in five minutes. Thank you both for your time. Please be safe.

To my family and friends who encouraged and inspired me.

To zombie fans keeping the genre alive.

A professional thank you for their advice:

Author G.B. Rich: [Instagram] GregTheWriter83

Author Nic Roads:
https://www.nicroads.com

Author Kevin Walsh
http://www.facebook.com/kevin.walsh.982?ref=tn_tnmn

Made in the USA
Las Vegas, NV
06 April 2024

88355536R00142